Jillian Dare

— A Novel —

Melanie M. Jeschke

Revell

a division of Baker Publishing Group
Grand Rapids, Michigan

© 2009 by Melanie M. Jeschke

Published by Revell
a division of Baker Publishing Group
P.O. Box 6287, Grand Rapids, MI 49516-6287
www.revellbooks.com

Printed in the United States of America

Library of Congress Cataloging-in-Publication Data
Jeschke, Melanie M., 1953–
    Jillian Dare : a novel / Melanie Jeschke.
      p. cm.
    ISBN 978-0-8007-3316-2 (pbk.)
    I. Title.
  PS3610.E83J55 2009
  813′.6—dc22   2009000548

To
my sister
Deborah Morey Holden
and
my sister-in-Christ
Inece Yvette Bryant

Look at the birds of the air; they do not sow or reap or store away in barns, and yet your heavenly Father feeds them. Are you not much more valuable than they? . . . But seek first his kingdom and his righteousness, and all these things will be given to you as well.

Matthew 6:26, 33

1

*L*ife is full of surprises: some kissed by joy, others stabbed by sorrow. My own life had experienced more of the latter in its brief span. I was, therefore, embarking on a new job and a new situation with an ambivalence borne of hopeful anticipation and cautious dread.

The first surprise on my journey was the deer that suddenly leaped out of the woods and across the roadway. I slammed on the brakes just in time to avoid hitting it. I must confess that my fear of auto accidents borders on phobic.

My little Honda Civic lurched and stalled.

"Great," I muttered as I fiddled with the ignition, and then I looked up. I sucked in my breath and exhaled loudly. "Oh my . . ."

Emerging from the tree-lined boulevard across a vast lawn, Carter Plantation sprawled before me—a gracious three-storied brick Federal mansion with a portico supported by white Doric columns. On either side of the central building spread identical two-storied wings in that perfect balance typical of the Georgian style.

What wasn't typical was the sheer size of it all. I couldn't recall ever seeing such a large house before—and I was on my way to work there. I had accepted a job as a nanny to Cadence Remington, a little toddler of thirteen months, an age I felt perfectly competent to manage. But this enormous house was more than I had bargained for. The image of Julie Andrews as Maria in *The Sound of Music*, cowed by her first glimpse of the von Trapp mansion, flashed into my mind. As I slipped my car into gear, I tentatively and then more boldly sang Maria's tune, "I have confidence in confidence alone!"

Driving up to the mansion, I recalled my job interview at the Strasbourg Inn just a week earlier when I had met a small elderly woman with soft white wooly hair and bright blue eyes. She looked as huggable as a lamb and smelled faintly of lilacs.

"You must be Jillian," she had said warmly, extending her hand.

I had grasped it firmly. "Mrs. Remington?" I asked with some confusion.

She laughed lightly—her laughter had a pleasant musical sound like wind chimes. "No, dear. I'm Mrs. Carter. I should have introduced myself. I'm Elise, Ethan Remington's aunt."

I hadn't meant to frown, but I must have looked puzzled

because Mrs. Carter added, "Ethan asked me to conduct the interview for him today. His work keeps him very busy. He's the founder and CEO of his own international company—Remington Telecommunications or RemTel—you've heard of it?"

I nodded.

"Much of his business is in the UK, so he travels quite a lot. His father was British, and the Remingtons still own an estate over in England."

This explained the enticing part of the job description I had read at the agency, calling for a nanny willing to travel to England. That was what had really appealed to me, a young woman who had never been farther away than the beaches of Delaware but who had, nevertheless, procured a passport just in case the opportunity to travel presented itself.

"You see," she continued to explain, "both of his parents have passed on, so everything has fallen on him. But with his business to run and two estates to manage, he really can't do it all on his own. It's just too much. That's why I'm tasked with the interview."

"And Mrs. Remington?"

Mrs. Carter shook her head mournfully. "I'm sorry to say Mrs. Remington is no longer with us."

"Oh, I'm so sorry," I murmured. *How dreadful for Mr. Remington to have lost so many loved ones!* "That's so sad for him and for his daughter."

"Yes, yes, it is very sad. A terrible business." She sighed heavily. "It's a mercy the baby is so young and doesn't know any better. Poor Ethan has been a single father practically since she was born, which is why we must have a full-time nanny. I'm just getting too old to be chasing a toddler around the house all day."

Mrs. Carter brightened. "Now if you decide to take the job, your contract states you will have afternoons and three evenings a week off, plus a full weekend every month. I'll try to give you lots of privacy, and I think you'll find your rooms quite nice. And you should know that Ethan is very generous to his staff. He'll pay your social security, health insurance, and your travel expenses. And he'll put money in an IRA for you too. We'll have the month trial period, but I do hope you'll be happy with us and everything works out."

She paused and went on cautiously, "I thought Caroline, our former nanny, was happy, but then she quit quite suddenly. I'm not sure why, but it left us high and dry."

"It all sounds perfect to me," I said. "But, Mrs. Carter, I'm sure you'd like to ask me some questions first."

"Oh yes, yes, of course. Now let me see . . ." She rummaged around in an enormous black handbag until she pulled out a crumpled piece of paper. "Here it is!" She laughed as if delighted with a wonderful discovery. "All of Ethan's questions."

And with that, Mrs. Carter conducted the interview and promptly hired me for a one-month trial period, which brought me to this moment of singing, "I have confidence in me!" as I pulled up to the portico of the mansion. I breathed a silent prayer, mounted the stairs with all the confidence I could muster, and rang the bell. I endured a very long wait while that confidence began to evaporate.

Suddenly the door swung wide and there stood Mrs. Elise Carter.

"Jillian!" she cried. "Do come in. I'm sorry to keep you waiting so long. We rarely use this door. We all park around back near the kitchen and come in that way."

"Oh, I'm sorry, Mrs. Carter. I can move my car."

"No, no. We can take care of that later. I'll ask Jack to move it and carry your things to your rooms. Now please come in and make yourself at home." She stepped back for me to enter and opened her arms in greeting. "Welcome to Carter Plantation, Jillian! We're so glad you're here."

"Thank you so much. I'm very happy to be here."

"Do you need to freshen up, my dear? There's a powder room just down the hall. And after that, could I get you something to drink? Some sweet tea, perhaps?"

I gratefully accepted both offers and was astonished that Mrs. Carter bustled about until I was comfortably sipping iced tea on the veranda under the portico roof. I wasn't certain what to expect on my arrival at Carter Plantation, but I hadn't expected to be treated as a guest.

Mrs. Carter settled into a wicker chair opposite mine. "There now. I love to sit out here when the weather's nice. Isn't this a grand view?"

I agreed that it was. The prospect looked over the gently sloping lawn to the boulevard lined with trees sporting their autumn cloaks of scarlet and orange against a brilliant azure sky. The periwinkle shadows of the Blue Ridge Mountains loomed in the distance beyond the rolling hills of Fauquier County in northern Virginia. Although it was October, the bright sun of an Indian summer afternoon spread along the veranda, and I lifted my face gratefully to its warmth.

"I never tire of this view," Mrs. Carter said cheerfully as she sipped her tea. "I was so blessed to marry into the Carter family. You know, Carter Plantation has been in this family for generations—ever since Robert 'King' Carter was granted about half of Virginia from King George II back in the colonial days."

Now I really was confused. "I thought Mr. Remington . . ."

Mrs. Carter's laughter chimed. "Oh, the estate does belong to Mr. Remington now, but it's still in the Carter family. You see, my sister-in-law was Ethan's mother. His full name is Ethan *Carter* Remington. Sadly, my dear husband and I were never blessed with children. So when George passed away, he willed the house to Ethan. But since Ethan travels so much, he's happy to leave me in charge here. And of course, he wants me here to look after Cadence while he's away."

"Mrs. Carter," I asked, "what is Cadence like? Could you please tell me a little more about her?"

"Oh yes! She's a darling, precious little girl." Her face lit up. "Very precocious and curious and absolutely delightful. She's very energetic, though, and I just can't keep up with her—even with Jack and his wife, Marta, to help. But Cadence is the joy of my life! Really, of everyone's life, especially Ethan's. My, how he dotes on her! By the way, Cadence is napping now. So you arrived at just the right time, because I'm quite at leisure to show you around the house."

Mrs. Carter rose, and I followed her about the mansion, trying to process all the information she poured forth as well as to orient myself so I would not lose my way later. The Carters had fastidiously maintained the integrity and elegance of the original Federal era structure. The more modern additions had every contemporary convenience without compromising the overall architectural harmony.

I could barely contain my delight when shown my own set of rooms. *My own rooms!* And not just one—but a suite complete with private bath, sitting room, and fully equipped kitchenette. Although I could enter the apartment from the main house, I also had my own separate entrance, which opened on to a patio overlooking the gardens in the back.

"We hope you'll take most of your meals with the family," Mrs. Carter was saying as I ran my hand over the shining teakettle in the kitchenette. "But if you prefer not to, especially on your evenings off, we've tried to make everything as comfortable as possible for you. Whatever suits you. By the way, Ethan has everything wired so that you have your own cable television and a laptop computer." She paused for a moment then asked almost anxiously, "So, Jillian, how do you like it?"

How could I explain to this sweet woman, who was so eager to please, that I could be satisfied with very little? Having grown up in a progression of foster homes, I had never had a room of my own—let alone an apartment. I looked around the cheerful, well-appointed au pair suite and exclaimed truthfully, "Oh, Mrs. Carter, I love it!"

"I'm so glad." She beamed at me with genuine pleasure. "There's one more thing. Let me show you how the security alarm works." Leading me over to a control panel, she demonstrated how to check that the system was operating.

I paid close attention. I was accustomed to living out in the country, but in the Shenandoah Valley, even the wealthiest people seldom locked their doors, and I mentioned something to that effect.

"I know, I know," Mrs. Carter replied. "We didn't lock our doors either when I lived here all those years with George. But after those teenagers murdered that doctor up in Loudoun County, Ethan insisted on putting in this system. If anyone tampers with the doors or windows, the police are automatically alerted. I suppose since he's gone so much, he worries about little Cadence."

She glanced down at her wristwatch. "Now we just have time for you to meet the household staff."

She led the way to the kitchen and introduced me to Jack and Marta Thornfield, an affable couple in their late fifties or early sixties, who managed the house and grounds and lived across the yard in a renovated cottage beside the garage and stables. Jack stood tall and wiry while Marta was plump and doughy. Jack Spratt and his wife—that's the mental image I could hang his name on. But Marta would be harder to remember. Mrs. Carter interrupted my thoughts, explaining that a cleaning crew as well as a gardener came in several times a week for the heavier chores.

As we chatted in the kitchen, a handsome black Labrador retriever rose from his bed near the stone fireplace and approached me, wagging his tail with friendly curiosity. He sniffed my shoes and I held out the back of my hand for him to investigate before venturing to pet him.

"This is Ranger, Ethan's dog," Mrs. Carter said.

"He's beautiful," I murmured as I ran my hand over his thick coat. "I love labs. They're so good-natured."

"Seems you meet with his approval too. I'm glad you like dogs. But we should finish our tour. It's time you met Cadence."

I followed her back to my wing of the house and the nursery suite next door to mine. She tapped lightly on the closed door and opened it to a playroom painted in bright primary colors. A pretty teenaged girl with straight shoulder-length blond hair slouched on a sofa. She looked up from her reading as we entered.

"Hello, Corinne," Mrs. Carter cheerfully greeted the girl. "Meet our new nanny, Jillian Dare. Jillian, this is our babysitter, Corinne Cooke. She comes over every weekday afternoon during the baby's naptime and keeps an eye on her until supper. That will give you a few hours every day to yourself."

"Hi, Corinne," I said. "Nice to meet you."

Corinne eyed me. Did I note a look of disdain or was it just bored indifference? I guessed she wouldn't be very impressed with my lack of stylishness. Although I was only a few years her senior, I had tamed my curly waist-length light brown hair by braiding it and twisting it into a neat bun. I had also carefully chosen my outfit to reflect a serious, mature professional. I wore a long gray jersey skirt and a modest royal blue sweater set, which would enhance the blue of my eyes. I'm never sure how to fill in the blank on forms requesting the color of my eyes. They are an indeterminate and constantly shifting color— gray, green, or blue. Like the color of the sea that reflects the sky, my eyes reflect what I'm wearing.

The babysitter grunted a return greeting and gathered up her schoolbooks, which had been scattered over the couch. "Should I wake up Cadence now?" she asked.

Mrs. Carter checked her watch. "Yes, dear. Why don't you? If she naps too late, we'll never get her to sleep tonight. Plus I'd like for Jillian to meet her."

While Corinne went into the adjoining room to wake the child, Mrs. Carter pointed out the amenities of the nursery suite. The layout was identical to mine with a kitchenette, but entirely childproofed and looking much like a well-equipped preschool. The playroom contained a child-sized table and chairs, a flat-screen television with a DVD player, and organized bins and shelves full of toys, puzzles, books, and craft supplies. Evidently a tremendous amount of thought and care had gone into designing this nursery suite.

Mrs. Carter mentioned that Mr. Remington's rooms connected to Cadence's bedroom, just as mine connected to the nursery sitting room.

"He likes to be able to check on her easily when he's home, but unfortunately he does travel a lot. You have a monitor in your apartment so that you can hear her if she should wake in the middle of the night, and we also have monitors throughout the house. Ah, here is our little darling!" she exclaimed as Corinne carried the toddler into the playroom.

And Cadence was a little darling—huge blue eyes, dark curly hair, and pudgy cheeks. At first she shyly hid her face in Corinne's shoulder, but when she was put down it only took a few minutes for her to warm up to me and to begin to bring me toy "gifts," plopping them in my lap.

She won my heart in no time, and I hoped that I would quickly win hers. The expense and consideration that had gone into her care made me wonder even more about her father and when I would be introduced to him. My curiosity about the owner of Carter Plantation would not be satisfied for another two weeks—and even after I met him, Mr. Remington remained a mystery to me for quite some time.

I actually first made his acquaintance in cyberspace. After dinner and Cadence's bedtime, I began to put away my few belongings and acclimate myself to my new rooms. Beside the computer, I discovered a set of instructions for activating my "nanny" email account. When I logged in, I was surprised to find two messages in the inbox. The first was from Ethan .Remington@RemTel.org, my boss and Cadence's father.

Dear Miss Dare:

Welcome to Carter Plantation. I am pleased you have

decided to take care of my daughter and trust we will work well together providing for her needs. I hope you have found everything to your satisfaction. Please let me know if there is anything lacking in your accommodation or provision. I plan to return to Virginia in a fortnight's time. In the meantime, feel free to contact me via email with any questions or concerns you may have. In case of emergency, you may call my mobile phone. My aunt has the number.

Best regards,

Ethan Remington

Although his email was appropriately businesslike in tone, I felt pleased that my new boss had been thoughtful enough not only to provide me with a computer and email account but also to be solicitous of my needs.

The second message also had the RemTel domain address. The sender's name appeared simply as CC. The subject line read "Nanny." Surprised, I decided I should open it. The three words all in capital letters on the otherwise blank page made my stomach flip.

WATCH YOUR BACK!

Instinctively, I whipped my head around. Of course, nobody was there. *How silly of me. But who would write such a thing? And how did they have my address?*

I rapidly hit the delete button and shut down the computer. Rising quickly, I slipped through the connecting door and crossed the nursery sitting room to check on Cadence. She was sleeping soundly, and the baby monitor seemed to be working properly. I locked her hallway door from the inside, and when I returned to my suite, I locked mine as well. Next, I tried the door to the outside patio to make sure it too was securely locked. After checking that the security alarm was working, I peered under the bed and in the closets and opened the shower curtain.

While I dressed for bed, I puzzled over the mystery message. *Who could CC be? So far I've met only Marta, Jack, and of course, Mrs. Carter. Could Elise Carter possibly be CC? She hardly seems the type to send threatening emails. But was it a threat or a warning? She mentioned that in the next county some teenagers had killed a doctor.* The thought of teenagers brought the babysitter Corinne to mind. *What's her last name? Cooke. Corinne Cooke. Could she be CC? And what about the former nanny—Caroline? Then again, there must be hundreds of employees who work for RemTel and have access to their email account. But why would anyone send me such a message?*

My mind whirled and I tried to reason myself out of my fears. Placing a flashlight and the phone within reach on my bed table, I left on a nightlight and lay on my back with the covers pulled up to my chin until I finally fell asleep.

2

The first two weeks of my trial period rapidly passed, and I determined that I loved my new position almost as much as my new charge. Little Cadence returned my affection in that trusting and guileless manner unique to toddlers. Having a little person love me unreservedly was always a welcome sensation. The rest of the household were amiable and pleasant. Like Mrs. Carter, they quickly accepted me into their "family" circle. The beauty of my surroundings and the amenities of my accommodations all contributed to my contentment and enjoyment.

Only a vague sense of isolation and perhaps a bit of ennui marred that contentment. Although friendly and kind, none of the other members of the household were my age. By circumstance, I had been lonely for much of my life; and yet, however accustomed I was to this, I had never acquiesced to it. Now the flashes of loneliness stirred a longing in my soul. They also caused me to spend much of my free time wondering about my employer and when I would be able to meet him. I was surprised and pleased that daily he thoughtfully left a brief message in my email inbox. I responded in turn with a report of what Cadence had done that day. I enjoyed our exchanges and looked forward to checking my email each evening.

A week passed with no more threatening correspondence from the mysterious CC. I had begun to relax into assuming the first missive had been a random spammer when the name suddenly popped up in my inbox. Again, it read "Nanny" in the subject line. With no little trepidation, I clicked to open it. An obscene word in capital letters flashed across the screen before I hurriedly punched the delete button.

Toward the end of the second week, the sender's name of CC surfaced again. I determined to delete it unopened and then realized that perhaps I should save it for evidence for Mr. Remington, so that he could take necessary disciplinary action. He would probably want to know that one of his employees was misusing the company domain.

I opened it.

YOU ARE BEING WATCHED!

I shuddered. It was all I could do to resist the impulse to erase the message. After some deliberation I decided to save it in a folder I dubbed "CC," which I could later show to Mr. Remington.

With the exception of these disconcerting communications and that vague sense of discontent borne from loneliness—and, I must confess, a curious desire to meet my employer—my new life at Carter Plantation was more than I could have wished for. I hoped that when Mr. Remington did return home, I would likewise meet his approval.

In the afternoons while Cadence slept under the care of the teenaged Corinne, I had a few hours to spend as I pleased. As an amateur photographer, I used some of my free time to take pictures of the mansion and surrounding countryside. Also an avid runner, I gave myself a good workout while exploring the estate at a more brisk pace. For me, little can surpass the sense of freedom and exhilaration of running outdoors; and whatever the weather, I have seldom missed an opportunity to follow my daily exercise regimen.

One brilliant afternoon following several days of steady rain, I set off down the long driveway, reveling in the bright sunshine sparkling on the damp grass. A few brave splashes of orange, yellow, and red still stubbornly clung to the trees. My feet thudded on the thick piles of spent, wet leaves underneath. The pungent smell of dank earth and decaying leaves mixed with the smoke of a wood fire drifting dreamily by. The comfortingly familiar and yet surprisingly poignant smells and sights of autumn in Virginia never ceased to delight me. After picking my way through a large pondlike puddle strewn with slick leaves, I finally hit my stride on the open drive, my long ponytail swinging back and forth like a metronome keeping time with my pace.

Suddenly a shiny black convertible burst into my view. I jumped clear of the road as it sped past me. Without slowing down, the driver turned to stare at me.

"You idiot!" I wanted to shout. *"Slow down and watch where you're going!"*

Perhaps I should have voiced my warning. A few seconds later, I watched and heard the screeching, skidding, and smashing of the car as the driver tried to brake at the large puddle but instead slid over the slick leaves and into the broad trunk of an ancient poplar tree. The air bag deployed with a loud pop.

I ran to the car and jerked open the driver's door. The booming voice of a radio talk show host greeted me.

"Are you all right, sir?" I asked above the din of the radio.

The driver mumbled something in reply. He appeared dazed but not bloodied. I reached my hand along the dashboard, found the keys, and switched off the ignition to avert the possibility of an explosion. That also silenced the radio.

"Are you all right, sir?" I repeated. "Should I run for some help? There's a house just down this drive. I could run there and get someone to help you. It would only take me a few minutes. Are you able to get out?"

"Blast this air bag!" The driver suddenly punched at it. "I think I'm all right, but who would know with this stupid thing in the way?"

"May I help you?"

He eyed me. "Bit small to be pulling a man out of a car, aren't you?"

His accent sounded different, but I couldn't quite place it. Surely he was not a Virginian, I thought, and as a stranger, he was even more in need of my assistance. I ignored his comment and tried again.

"May I help you? Try grabbing my arm and let's see if it will give you enough leverage to get out."

He grunted but did as I suggested. I braced myself with one hand on the car roof while offering him the other. I pulled while he pushed himself out of his seat with his right arm. After a brief struggle, we were triumphant.

"Thank you," he said simply, brushing off his khaki Dockers trousers and smoothing his navy blue Ralph Lauren polo shirt. He straightened up and smiled. He had the most even and white teeth I had seen in a good long while. It was a nice smile. He looked like he could be a model for a toothpaste commercial, or for anything, for that matter. I don't normally put much stock in a person's appearance, but the attractiveness of this unknown driver completely disconcerted me. He appeared powerfully built with broad shoulders, and I judged he stood about five feet ten or eleven. Although not classically handsome, his features were regular and pleasant, framed by thick, raven black hair, which seemed professionally cut and styled. Heavy black eyebrows furrowed over dark chocolate brown eyes.

I realized those eyes were scrutinizing me, and I instinctively dropped my gaze. "Are you all right, sir? I live just down the road and can run home for help."

"You live down the road? Where?" he demanded.

"At Carter Plantation."

He scowled as if incredulous. "At Carter Plantation?"

"Yes, I'm the nanny there."

"Ah! The nanny." The scowl lifted. "Of course."

"Would you like me to go for some help?"

"No. I have my mobile." He paused and then added, "But thank you. Now excuse me a moment." He tapped in a number while I stepped back discreetly to afford him some privacy. I considered continuing on my run, but concluded I should wait to be sure he would receive the help he needed.

After a brief conversation, he snapped shut his phone and ruefully examined the crushed fender of his black car, a well-cared-for and expensive model despite the damage. I noted the emblem: Lamborghini.

"Blast it all," he muttered. Glancing at me standing quietly by, he raised his voice. "I've called for help, so you needn't stay."

"That's all right. I'll just wait until someone arrives. I'd like to be sure you're all right."

"That's nice of you, but you shouldn't feel guilty about causing the accident."

"Causing the accident?" I sputtered. "How did I cause it?"

"You startled me—just popping out on the drive like that."

The nerve of the man!

"Excuse me, sir, but you were speeding on a private road and you weren't watching where you were going. That's hardly my fault. I'm sorry you had an accident and that your car is damaged, but you really should be more careful. Mr. Remington would not approve of someone driving recklessly on his property."

He laughed—rather rudely and sardonically, to my thinking. "Mr. Remington?"

"Yes," I said, feeling oddly defensive. "Mr. Remington. The owner of this property, Carter Plantation."

"And do you know Mr. Remington well, that you can represent his opinions?"

"No," I admitted. "I haven't met him yet. But I daresay he would not want anyone speeding on his drive."

He chuckled. "No, I'm sure he wouldn't—especially if they were to crash into this fine old poplar. Ah, here comes my help."

A pickup truck, which I recognized as Jack's, pulled up. Ranger, barking loudly, bounded out of the truck bed and over to the driver, whom he greeted joyously.

"Hey, old boy," the man said, stooping to fondle the dog's ears. "Did you miss me? Have you been taking good care of baby Cadence?" He dropped his voice at the end of each question as if he were making a statement.

And then I recognized that inflection. He was British.

He looked up as Jack hurried over to the wrecked car. "Hello, Jack. Fine kettle of fish, eh?"

A dawning realization caused me to regret that I had not followed my first impulse to continue on my run.

"Thank God you're all right!" Jack said and then he noticed me. "Jillian, what are you doing here?"

"Miss Dare was out jogging and gave me quite a fright, which caused me to hit this puddle and skid into the tree," the driver replied for me. "So she determined to set things right by staying here until I was rescued. That's correct, isn't it, Miss Dare?" He challenged me with his eyes.

At that moment I fervently wished that the earth would open and swallow me whole, but I stubbornly held my ground.

"Not entirely," I replied. "But I am sorry about your accident, sir."

"No lasting harm done," he said. "And accidents do happen. Especially when one is speeding on a private road. Forgive me for not introducing myself, Miss Dare."

He offered his hand.

"I'm Ethan Remington."

3

After that humiliating introduction to my employer, I decided to finish my run, take a shower, and change my clothes in case my presence was required. But I planned to prepare my own supper so that I could avoid further contact if possible.

It was not possible.

Mrs. Carter buzzed me on the house intercom and informed me that Mr. Remington had requested that Cadence and I join them for dinner in the dining room at seven o'clock. I dressed in the long gray skirt and the royal blue sweater set that I had worn on my first day at Carter Plantation. Plaiting my hair, I twisted it into a neat bun, allowing a few wisps to curl around my ears. I relieved Corinne of Cadence's care and changed the baby into a sweet rosebud smocked dress before carrying her to the dining room and securing her in an antique high chair. After tying a bib around Cadence's neck, I gave her some milk in a sippy cup and sat down to wait.

I did not wait long. As the grandfather clock in the foyer chimed the hour of seven, Mrs. Carter and Mr. Remington appeared in the dining room. Cadence babbled with excitement. Mr. Remington kissed her with obvious affection. He then nodded to me while seating his aunt. After he said the blessing, Marta served us the meal, and we began to eat.

Our preliminary dinner conversation consisted of requests for items to be passed and polite comments on the weather. And then came the topic I had been dreading.

"Ethan," Mrs. Carter said, "Marta told me that you were in an accident today. What on earth happened?"

"Well, Auntie, I'm afraid that I saw an elven maiden flitting along the side of the road, and I was so astonished that I lost control of the car and crashed into a tree."

"Really, Ethan! What do you mean, you saw an elven maiden? You've been watching those *Lord of the Rings* movies again, haven't you?"

"If only I had the time for that, dear aunt. No, the sad truth is that I was speeding, and I hit a big puddle and some wet leaves and then skidded off the road."

I looked up sharply and was surprised when he caught my eye and winked. *So, he really isn't blaming me after all.*

"Honestly, Ethan, you should be more careful," Mrs. Carter chided him. "You weren't hurt, were you?"

"No, I'm fine. Just a little bruised from the air bag."

"And your car?"

"I crumpled the fender, but it's easy enough to repair. No real harm done."

"Thank God for that."

"Yes," he agreed. "So, Miss Dare," he said, turning his attention to me. "Tell me something about yourself. If you don't mind my saying so, you seem very young to be out in the work world. Are you really twenty?"

"Yes, sir."

"You may drop the 'sir.' I may be quite a bit older than you, but even so, I'd prefer not to be pegged a 'sir.' You make me feel positively decrepit."

"Yes, sir." *That was stupid!* I could feel a blush creeping up my neck.

"Ah, ah!" he chided.

"Yes, Mr. Remington." Flustered, I looked down at my plate.

He sighed. "You may call me Ethan if you like."

I wasn't sure I really felt comfortable with that, but I didn't want to appear difficult either. "Thank you. And I go by Jillian."

"Right. Now, Jillian, where are you from?"

"The Harrisonburg area in the Shenandoah Valley."

"And your family is still in Harrisonburg?"

"I don't have any family."

"No family?" His manner softened. "You're an orphan?"

I remembered he had lost both his parents. "Not really. I

never knew who my parents were. They could be alive, but I wouldn't know. I was abandoned—left as a newborn at the Rockingham County Hospital."

"Abandoned," he repeated under his breath. "Poor girl." He glanced over at Cadence, who was busy playing with her food and on occasion smearing some into her mouth. His attention returned to me. "How did you come to be given the name of 'Dare'?"

"The nurses chose it for me. They named me for Virginia Dare, the first settler baby to be born in the New World. My full name is Jillian Virginia Dare."

"Why Jillian?"

"That was the name of the nurse who found me."

"So, did this nurse adopt you?"

"No. My first set of foster parents planned to, but they were killed in an automobile accident. After that I lived in a succession of foster homes."

"Your entire life?" He frowned. "Were you well treated?"

"Not for the most part. To be honest, my upbringing was rather Dickensian." I said this matter-of-factly because it was true, not because I was asking for sympathy.

Nevertheless, I saw sympathy in Mr. Remington's eyes.

He asked, "Were you in any good homes?"

"A few. And for the last several years, I was blessed to live with a good family called the Brookes, who have eight children. That's where I honed my babysitting skills."

"*Eight* children?" he repeated with surprise. "Are they Mormons or Catholics?"

I smiled, as I had often heard this question. "No, but they are Christians."

"So tell me, Jillian, did living with all those children make you decide to be a nanny?"

"I certainly received a lot of practical experience dealing with children when I lived with them. I found I was good with little ones, especially babies."

"But wouldn't you like to go on to a university and earn a degree?"

"I might want to some day, but for now I thought it would be good to have some practical job experience. I also want to save some money so that I can afford to go to college later if I decide to. But the truth is that I love children and really would prefer to be a nanny at this point in my life. Besides," I added, "I would like to give to children what I never had—a mother figure, if you will, to love and care for them."

"Hmm, I see."

Mrs. Carter chimed in. "I think that's wonderful. Very admirable of you, Jillian, to turn your misfortune into something good. And she is good with children, Ethan. I've noticed how well she does with Cadence."

Mr. Remington nodded. "I'm glad to hear that. I thought as much from your email reports. By the way, Jillian, I appreciated hearing from you. It was considerate of you to keep me informed. So now that you've finished a fortnight of your trial period, do you think you will want to stay with us?"

"Oh yes!" I said. "I mean, if it suits you."

"I believe it does, although we will all have to reevaluate

when the month is up. But tell me more about yourself. Do you often go out running?"

"Yes, I try to get out every day," I replied.

"So you like to keep fit. And what else do you do in your free time? Any other interests other than running? Do you like to read?"

"Yes, I do."

"What sorts of books?"

Now this is a subject I can warm up to. "All sorts, really," I replied with enthusiasm. "I guess my favorites are historical novels and the classics."

"Who are your favorite authors?"

"I'd say Charles Dickens, Charlotte Brontë, and Jane Austen."

"So then—are you a *Pride and Prejudice* fan?"

"I am."

He smiled mischievously. "Or are you really more of a Colin Firth fan?"

Now I was puzzled. "Colin Firth?"

"You know—the actor who played Darcy in the *Pride and Prejudice* miniseries. All the ladies seem to go for him."

"I'm sorry, I don't know him. I don't watch much television."

"You don't know Colin Firth?" interjected Mrs. Carter. "My, he is *so* handsome as Darcy and *so* romantic! I love the way he broods over Elizabeth Bennett. If only I were younger . . ."

I shook my head.

"You mean you haven't watched the A&E version of *Pride and Prejudice* like every other woman of my acquaintance?" asked Mr. Remington.

"I'm afraid not. The family I lived with last didn't have a TV."

"You're joking! Are they Amish?"

I smiled again and repeated, "No, just Christians. The Brookes had a theory that if they didn't watch TV, their children would read more. The father said that the children could either watch TV or be on TV by being successful, and he preferred the latter."

"Interesting perspective. Have you been to the cinema then? Do you ever watch films?"

"Of course."

"So you don't object on religious grounds to watching movies?"

"No. I love watching movies. In fact, I have seen the film version of *Pride and Prejudice*."

"I'm glad to hear it."

Mrs. Carter added with undisguised pride, "Ethan is a film producer, you know."

"Really?"

He shook his head. "Nothing to be impressed about, I assure you. I just put up the money. Mostly for small, independent British films. So, Jillian," he said directing the conversation back to me, "you enjoy running, reading good books, and occasionally watching a good film. What else do you like to do in your spare time? Any hobbies?"

"Why, yes, I do have one."

"And that would be?"

"Photography. Last year I was able to take a class at Valley Community College and I loved it."

"Really? What sort of pictures do you like to take?"

"I like to photograph nature as well as people. And interesting architecture too. Anything that captures my attention, really."

"Do you use film or a digital camera?"

"I prefer film—but that's the kind of camera I have."

"You don't have a digital camera?"

"Not yet. Perhaps I'll buy one after I've worked for a while. But like I said, I prefer film anyway."

"Do you have any of your photographs here?"

"Yes, I do."

"As soon as dinner is finished, go get them. I'd like to see them." He paused and with some effort added in a less officious tone, "Please. If I may."

"Of course, that would be fine."

When Marta came in to serve dessert and coffee, I excused myself from the table and walked briskly to my suite for my portfolio. I brought them to Mr. Remington's place at the dinner table and laid them gently by his coffee. He examined them carefully. I don't know why, but I had the queerest sensation in my stomach while he scrutinized my work.

He held up several photos I had taken of Cadence. "These are rather good," he murmured as if surprised.

"Thank you."

"It's quite remarkable how you've captured her mischievous side as well as her sweetness. And your use of light is inspired. Plus I really like the composition of these pictures of Carter Plantation," he said, perusing a sheaf of photographs of the mansion and the grounds. "I'd like to buy these from you."

"Oh, you don't need to buy them. You may just keep them."

"No, I will buy them. After all, you had to pay for the film and developing. And your time and creativity are worth something too. Have you ever sold any of your pictures?" he asked as he looked through a series of trees decked in their blazing fall foliage.

"No, sir."

"I really think you should consider doing so. I know a shopkeeper in Middleburg who could do quite well in selling these for you if you like."

"That would be incredible!"

"Good. If I may hold on to these a while longer, I'll take them to her and see what she says."

"Thank you, sir . . . um . . . Mr. Remington . . . I mean . . ."

His mouth crooked in a thin smile. "Never mind." He glanced over at the baby, who was straining to squirm out of the safety belt of her high chair. "Cadence seems ready to get down now," he observed. "I think it's her bedtime."

"Yes, sir," I said automatically and rose quickly from the table.

"I'll be along in a little while to check on her," he announced.

"Yes, Mr. Remington. Please excuse us." I realized my second faux pas and grimaced as I wiped the baby's hands and face and picked her up.

"I hope you are not offended by all my questions, Jillian," he said when we reached the doorway.

"No, not at all. You have every right to know all about me. I don't mind, really. You should ask me lots of questions. Not just because you are my employer but because you have entrusted your most precious possession to me."

His dark eyes traveled from my face to that of the baby resting on my hip. Those eyes conveyed a deep sorrow. "Yes, she is my most precious possession," he replied wistfully. "She is my pearl of great price."

After I bathed Cadence and dressed her for bed, I warmed up a bottle of milk for her. She had an endearing habit of caressing a lock of my hair while she drank from her bottle. If my hair were up in a bun, she would grab at me and cry until I let it down so that she could reach a strand. I wondered if her mother had had long hair and if this habit had been borne from some early bonding with that poor woman. And poor baby! To lose her mother at such a young age that she would never remember her. I felt such empathy for this little one. Whenever she stroked my hair, as she did this night, it warmed my heart, yet saddened it too.

I sang softly an old lullaby as I rocked her.

"Hush little baby, don't say a word. Papa's gonna buy you a mockingbird. If that mockingbird don't sing, Papa's gonna buy you a diamond ring."

There was a gentle tap on the door, and Mr. Remington stood in the doorway. He had an odd look on his face, which I couldn't decipher, and he made no movement to enter, as if he hesitated to interrupt. But hearing him, Cadence turned her head and then releasing my hair, struggled to sit up.

"I'm sorry to ruin such a pretty picture," he said.

"Not at all. She wants you to take her. Would you like to sit here while she finishes her bottle?"

I arose so that he could use the rocking chair. He didn't need much persuasion. "All right," he said as he held out his arms to his daughter. She dove into them and was soon back to busily sucking on her bottle.

We didn't speak. There was no need. He was absorbed by his child. I quietly straightened up the nursery and signaled that I would be next door if wanted. He nodded and returned his affectionate gaze on the baby.

Back in my room, I decided to go online to email Sharon, my closest friend from the Brookes clan. When I clicked on my inbox, a message from CC flashed on the screen. Although it sickened me to do so, I opened it. It read:

DON'T TRUST HIM!

4

Don't trust him.
I'll admit the warning haunted me over the next few weeks.

Since Mr. Remington was now home and his rooms connected to Cadence's, I thought it prudent to begin locking the door between her room and mine after I put her to bed. I kept the intercom on in case she did awaken during the night. She was a sound sleeper, however, and thankfully rarely stirred.

Don't trust him.

But it was difficult not to trust him, and why should I listen to CC anyway? Wasn't he or she the one not to trust? At least it seemed so to me. Everything about Mr. Remington spoke trust to my heart. He was affectionate and attentive to his daughter, kind in his regard to his aunt and staff, diligent in his care of his company and his estate, and even solicitous of my needs. He appeared to me to be everything one could hope for in an employer.

And I'll admit there was more. I have already described him as not being classically handsome. Perhaps there are some who might not even find him attractive, and he was, in fact, quite a bit older than I. But he had such a contagious vivacity, such a magnetic personality, and such a beautiful smile that I found him exceedingly attractive indeed.

I knew I was in danger of developing a severe crush on him.

His moods shifted often, and when I encountered him by chance about the house, I could never be certain whether I would be greeted with that engaging smile or with a glowering scowl. His changes in mood did not trouble me, however, any more than shifts in the weather would. I understood that I was of little consequence to him—other than in my role as Cadence's nanny—and that his scowls were not personally directed to me. I found it rather diverting to wonder what could be their cause or, if given the opportunity, how I might be able to steer him toward happier thoughts.

With the arrival of Mr. Ethan Remington, the atmosphere at Carter Plantation changed dramatically. Everything became livelier. The staff bustled about preparing meals, cleaning the house, and sprucing up the grounds. The telephone rang frequently while visitors came and went. Mr. Remington dropped into the nursery several times a day to check on Cadence, and we were invited to join him for dinner every evening when he was home. After completing my month trial period, I was pleased to accept his offer to stay on. One day I realized that my ennui had lifted.

Don't trust him.

But how could I not? And yet the warning had planted a seed of doubt, which held me back from sharing with him my file of emails from CC. Who could this CC be? Corinne Cooke hardly seemed likely. Although her disdain for me was thinly disguised, it appeared to be rooted merely in a sort of snobbery. I didn't sense any malevolence behind it. Clearly, I was not "cool" enough for her taste. She genuinely cared for Cadence and treated me with civility; therefore, I was satisfied with our working relationship. No, there was no indication that CC could be Corinne.

And for a time the mysterious messages stopped so that I was almost able to put them out of my mind.

One morning shortly after I had returned from spending Thanksgiving with the Brooke family, Mr. Remington stopped by the nursery to play with Cadence before lunch. He had come from a business breakfast and still sported a suit although he had loosened his tie and undone the top button of his shirt.

"Good morning, ladies!" He scooped Cadence up in his arms, tossed her in the air, and gently caught her. She chortled as he smothered her in kisses.

I grabbed my camera from the counter of the kitchenette and snapped away. Mr. Remington put Cadence down and dropped on his knees to her level.

"What are you playing with today, darling girl? Puzzles?"

She dove onto her stomach to examine the large wooden puzzle pieces lying on the carpet. He followed suit, then glanced up as I took another picture.

"You don't mind, do you?" I asked, lowering the camera.

"Of course not. As long as I get first dibs at seeing them and buying any I fancy. Cadence is a pretty little subject, isn't she?"

"Yes, she is."

"And what about me, Jillian? Do you find me a handsome subject?" He flashed his beautiful smile.

I almost choked. Yes, I did find him quite handsome indeed, but I wasn't about to confess that to him. He had me trapped. I always tell the truth. I decided it would be prudent to skirt the question. "I think that you have a very interesting face that photographs well."

He laughed. "That's a polite way of saying that I'm not handsome. Don't worry, I know I'm not."

I wanted to argue but thought it best to remain silent.

He gave a puzzle piece to Cadence. "Cow," he said. "Cow. Where does the cow go?" He guided her chubby hand to the appropriate spot and applauded her as she plopped it in. "That's right. Good girl. Now what does a cow say?"

"Moo!" she squeaked.

"Moo!" he bellowed back, and Cadence pealed with laughter. He tickled her, and she laughed even louder.

I am pleased to say that I took some very nice pictures.

He glanced at his watch and then up at me. "Jillian, could you two be ready to go out to lunch in thirty minutes? I'm meeting my solicitor at the Red Fox Tavern in Middleburg and would like Cadence to come along."

"Yes, sir. I can have her ready." I swallowed. "But are you sure you want to bring a toddler to a business lunch with your lawyer?"

"No problem. He's also one of my closest friends. It's been a while since he's seen Cadence, so I'd like her to come. She'll be fine—especially with you there." He stood up and brushed off his trousers. "We'll take the nanny mobile. Have her in her car seat by twelve sharp." He hesitated and then added, "Please."

❧

Mr. Remington is not one to be kept waiting. I barely had time to change Cadence's diaper, put her in a sweet plaid flannel dress, refill her sippy cup, and then change from my nanny uniform of khaki pants and a white polo shirt into my long gray skirt and a teal sweater. I zipped Cadence into a fleece jacket and left her in Marta's arms while I warmed up the Cadillac Escalade. I had her buckled in her car seat just as Mr. Remington emerged from the house.

"I'll drive," he said, getting in.

I shut Cadence's door and went around to the opposite side to climb into the seat beside her.

er effort.

He looked over his shoulder. "No, you don't have to ride back there. She's not fussing. You may sit up front." Leaning over, he opened the front door, and I slid into the passenger seat and fastened the shoulder harness.

"Have you been to Middleburg?" he asked as he sped down the long driveway and the avenue of poplar trees where I had first met him.

"Yes, I've been a few times on errands with Mrs. Carter."

"Did she take you to the Red Fox?"

"No, sir."

"Well, I think you'll enjoy it. Plus I have a little surprise for you."

He switched on the radio and left me to wonder. We drove by acres of rolling pasturelands divided by neat white fences. Horses grazed unperturbed by the passing traffic. The grand estates with their impressive stables gradually gave way to a more village-like collection of houses and shops, and Mr. Remington slowed down as we entered Middleburg. After parking in the lot behind the Red Fox Tavern, he hopped out of the car to assist me with Cadence.

"Should I bring the stroller?" I asked.

"No, I'll carry her," he replied, hoisting her to his shoulder.

I grabbed the diaper bag and followed him past the entrance to the Red Fox. Even with his little bundle, he walked briskly, and I quickened my pace as he held open the door to a gift shop. The decoupage sign read "Cachet."

The store smelled of cinnamon and cedar chips. An indoor

fountain flowed soothingly to the discreetly piped-in melodies of Mozart. Unique and beautiful objects were displayed with élan. If I had been by myself, I would have enjoyed browsing in such a store.

Mr. Remington strode purposefully to the back wall to view the collection of framed paintings and photographs.

"There, you see?" His voice held an air of satisfaction as he pointed to a small sign. In lovely calligraphy it read "Local Artist: Jillian Dare."

My photographs!

A fashionably dressed woman with frosted hair came from behind the counter to greet us. "Ethan! How are you? And Cadence. She's getting so big!"

"Hello, Evelyn. I'd like you to meet Jillian Dare, our nanny and budding photographer. Jillian, this is Evelyn Sullivan, the shop owner who has agreed to display your pictures."

Evelyn extended her well-manicured hand. "How nice to meet you, Jillian. I love your work! We've already sold a couple of your photos of Carter Plantation. Can you print up some more?"

"Why, yes, of course," I replied.

"Wonderful. And if you have new ones, I'd be happy to take a look at them. I'll send you a check for the ones that sold."

This *was* a surprise.

"Thank you very much," I said.

"Right. Well done," Mr. Remington said, glancing at his watch. "Sorry to have to run, but we have a reservation in five minutes. Thanks, Evelyn. We'll be in touch. By the way, if you can get that check out this week, it would be nice as we'll be leaving for England soon and Jillian may want to make some purchases before we go."

Leaving for England? Another surprise.

"Sure thing, Ethan. I'll put it in the mail tomorrow."

"Excellent. Thanks. Cheers!"

Taking a last lingering look at my photographs and my name on the sign, I followed him out of the store.

"So, how do you like being a local artist?" he asked over his shoulder.

"It's amazing. I didn't really expect you to pursue this for me. Thank you."

"You're welcome. But you should always expect me to pursue things. That's what I do."

"Mr. Remington, are we really going to England soon?" I had given up on trying to call him "Ethan" and he no longer corrected me.

"Yes, I'm sorry. I should have told you. Next week, in fact. You do have your passport?"

"Yes, sir. But you said something about needing to purchase some things?"

"Right. I wasn't sure if you have a proper suitcase, and you may need some more clothes. You'll have occasion to wear more than your nanny khakis. You know, Jillian, that teal sweater looks lovely on you and really enhances the green in your eyes, but I hope you don't mind me asking if that gray skirt of yours is the only one you have."

"The only skirt?"

"Right. I've noticed that you've worn it quite a bit."

He had noticed me. I felt a blush sweep up my neck and over my cheeks. "Yes, sir. I'm afraid it is my only skirt."

"Ah, I thought as much. You should probably go shopping with Aunt Elise before the trip. I'll give you a wardrobe allowance."

"Thank you. That's very nice of you, but it isn't necessary. I haven't had many expenses and have been saving my money. Plus now I'll get a little extra for the photos."

"But I insist on giving you a wardrobe allowance. We'll call it a travel bonus."

I already felt that traveling to England would be bonus enough, but I knew better than to argue with Mr. Remington once he had made up his mind about something.

A doorman welcomed us into the Red Fox Tavern. We walked across solid varnished hardwood planks that dated from the colonial era. Framed prints of foxes and horses graced the paneled walls, reminding me that this had been a favorite inn of Jackie Kennedy in her fox-hunting days. The place whispered of old money. The hostess addressed Mr. Remington by name and ushered us to a table where a high chair awaited Cadence, close to a cheery fire blazing away in a large stone fireplace.

A tall man with short, curly black hair, high cheekbones, and a brilliant smile rose to greet us. He was strikingly handsome and reminded me of the actor Denzel Washington. He and Mr. Remington clasped arms in a manly embrace before he bent to kiss Cadence. Mr. Remington introduced him to me as his lawyer, Calvin Cole.

Could he possibly be CC?

While Mr. Cole firmly grasped my hand, I studied his dark brown eyes. He met my gaze with friendly warmth. I could discern no trace of wariness or bitterness.

No, surely not.

I was prepared to sit at a separate table with Cadence, but the gentlemen invited me to join them. Mr. Remington politely pulled out a chair for me after I had settled the baby in her high chair.

"Well, Calvin," Mr. Remington said, "you're looking very fit and well rested. Did you have a good trip to Jamaica?"

"It was fantastic. Perfect weather and very relaxing. I managed not to check my email or voicemail messages the entire week. But of course, now I'm madly having to play catch-up at the office."

"How are your grandmother and the rest of the family doing?"

"Really well, thank you. Everyone is healthy and thriving. You should come down with me sometime, Ethan. You could use a little sun."

"I'll keep that in mind this winter," Mr. Remington said.

I entertained Cadence by giving her tiny Cheerios while we ordered and waited to be served. I was grateful that she cooperated and did not cause any disruptions to the hushed refinement surrounding us. I ordered a grilled cheese sandwich and milk for her and a Caesar salad with roasted chicken strips and peach iced tea for me. The men selected steak and red wine. Mr. Cole asked me a few polite questions about myself, how I was settling into my job, and how Cadence was adapting.

When the food arrived, the men launched into a variety of subjects: business, politics, and sports. I listened quietly. They spoke easily from long acquaintance. When they disagreed—particularly about politics—their words became heated and then dissipated into a truce of laughter. During a lull in the conversation while the waiter served coffee, I ventured a question.

"Excuse me, but would you mind telling me where you two met? You seem to have known each other for a long time."

Mr. Remington chuckled. "It has been a long time, hasn't it, Cal? To a young lady like Jillian, we must seem like old geezers."

Mr. Cole smiled. "We have known each other for well over a decade." He turned to me. "We were classmates at Yale."

Yale?

"You seem surprised, Jillian," Mr. Remington observed. "You don't think Calvin and I could have graduated from Yale?"

"No, it's not that. I had just assumed that you had gone to college in England."

"Well, you assumed correctly. I did take my degree in economics and management from Oxford, but received my MBA from Yale, which is where I met Calvin." He leaned closer to me and dropped his voice. "Jillian, do you think you might take Cadence to the ladies room to wash her up? I have a legal matter I need to discuss with Calvin in private."

"Of course." I quickly rose and extracted Cadence from her high chair. "Please excuse us."

I retrieved the diaper bag and headed off to the restroom, where I took my time changing Cadence and cleaning up the vestiges of her lunch clinging to her hair.

When I returned, the men had vacated the table and were arguing intensely in the foyer. A scowl clouded Mr. Remington's face. They abruptly broke off their conversation when they sighted me. Mr. Cole graciously said good-bye and kissed Cadence. He placed his hand on Mr. Remington's shoulder.

"I'm sorry, Ethan," he said.

On the ride home, Mr. Remington did not speak. I wondered what he and Mr. Cole could have discussed that had so upset him.

Perhaps Calvin Cole could be CC after all.

5

The thought that Mr. Cole could be the mysterious CC occurred to me again a few days later when he stayed ensconced with Mr. Remington in his home office for several hours. I saw them in the foyer on my way out for my afternoon run. As Mr. Cole departed, Mr. Remington appeared to be in a very dark mood indeed. I couldn't help being perplexed as to the cause, but it was certainly not my place to pry. Still, I did not like to see Mr. Remington upset.

Plans proceeded for our impending departure to the UK. The check for my photographs arrived as promised from Cachet, but Mr. Remington still insisted on giving me a shopping spree for a travel bonus. Armed with his credit card and a specific list of clothing required for the trip, Mrs. Carter drove me on a Saturday morning to Tyson's Corner shopping mall in the Washington, DC, suburb of Fairfax County. She wisely elicited the fashion aid of Corinne Cooke while Mr. Remington himself took care of Cadence for the day.

I do not enjoy shopping, but because I did not want to disappoint Mr. Remington, who was clearly going to a great deal of trouble for me, I gamely tried to cooperate. After growing up in the Shenandoah Valley, where most of my shopping had been at Wal-Mart, I found Tyson's Corner overwhelming—so many stores, so many customers, so much affluence and merchandise. Fortunately, Corinne knew just where to go. She understood intuitively that I would not want to wear anything too trendy or immodest, and led us directly to a conservative dress shop for petites.

"Buy black," she recommended. "It will travel well, and that's what everyone in London wears anyway, so you'll blend right in. Plus you can mix and match all your tops."

That suited me just fine.

"Now, dear," said Mrs. Carter, "don't even check the price tags. That's not your concern. What size do you wear? You're such a little thing. Corinne, you were so smart to bring us here. But I can't believe how tiny all these clothes are. I couldn't even get my right arm in one of these dresses!"

"You look about a size 4, is that right?" Corinne appraised me and began sorting through the racks. "We can just bring you clothes to try in the dressing room if you'd like."

The posh dressing rooms were a far cry from those at Wal-Mart, and even better, I had a personal shopper in Corinne. This turned out not to be such a traumatic experience after all. After a few tries, we found several pairs of slacks, a long skirt, and a pantsuit—all in black. We·had a little more difficulty finding a black cocktail dress that was modest, but the salesclerks joined in the hunt and succeeded. Corinne added color in a variety of wisely chosen machine-washable blouses, sweater sets, and tops in sky blue, periwinkle, turquoise, pink, and Christmas red. She then picked out some pretty scarves for accessories. I was stunned when Mrs. Carter also urged me to purchase a soft calfskin leather coat at Mr. Remington's specific request. He had insisted I would need a warm waterproof coat for the damp British winter. I felt awed by his consideration and generosity.

How could I *not* trust him?

I spent the next few days packing my suitcase as well as Cadence's. On the evening before our departure when all had been prepared and Cadence tucked into bed, I logged on to my email account to update my friends Sharon and Diane Brooke on the trip plans and purchases. I had been relieved that CC had been quiet for some time. The silence did make me wonder if Corinne had been the culprit after all and had since been won over.

As I sent off my letter to my friends, five new messages arrived in my inbox.

All from CC. My stomach knotted. I dreaded opening them but felt I must.

Again, each one was brief, each was written all in capital letters, and each sickened me.

The first read: I HATE YOU

The second: TRAVEL IS DANGEROUS

The third: WATCH OUT IN LONDON

The fourth: YOU ARE NOT SAFE

And the fifth and most frightening: THE BABY IS NOT SAFE

That did it. I had to tell Mr. Remington.

I tightly tied the belt of my flannel bathrobe and, unlocking the door between our rooms, first checked on Cadence. She was sprawled on her back, sleeping soundly in her crib. The door connecting her room to Mr. Remington's stood ajar. I could hear him pacing back and forth, opening and shutting drawers. Clearly, he was busy packing.

Hesitating only a moment, I drew up my courage and knocked lightly on the door.

"Mr. Remington?" I called softly.

He had a stack of starched and folded dress shirts in his hands. "Jillian? Is anything wrong?" He quickly placed the shirts on his bed and came to me. "Is it Cadence?"

"Cadence is fine," I whispered. "She's asleep. I'm sorry to bother you, especially now, but there's something I must show you. Could you spare just a few minutes?"

"Now?"

"Yes. I'm sorry. But it could be important."

"All right."

He followed me through the nursery to my au pair suite.

"I've been receiving some very strange emails on my Rem-Tel account and thought you should see them," I said as I sat down at my computer desk to bring them up. My hands trembled.

54

"You're frightened, aren't you? What sort of emails are they?"

I clicked on each one as he leaned over me to read. He drew in his breath sharply.

When we got to the fifth one, he gave an involuntary cry. "The baby? God have mercy!"

I fought back tears. "I'm so sorry, sir. I should have shown these to you before, but this is the first time there has been any threat to Cadence."

Mr. Remington turned my chair to face him. "What do you mean, Jillian? You have received other emails like this?"

I nodded. "Since my very first day here at Carter Plantation. They've all been from this CC using the RemTel provider."

"Did you save them?"

"Not at first, but then I thought I should in case they were from an employee of yours."

"Why didn't you tell me about them before now?"

"Well, in the beginning I thought they could have been some sort of prank and then—I don't know. And then I didn't get any for a while."

"May I read the ones you saved?"

"Yes, sir." I opened the CC folder. When he clicked on the message reading "Don't trust him!" I blushed. He didn't say anything, but I knew he knew why I hadn't told him before.

"I've been trying to figure out who CC is," I said. "I wondered if it could be Corinne Cooke or . . ." I hesitated. "You don't think it could be Mr. Cole, do you?"

"Calvin? No, no, not at all. Corinne, perhaps, but not Calvin." He was quiet for a few minutes. "I'll check into this. Meanwhile, we're going to shut down this account. We can open another one in your name or you can devise an account name of your choosing. Does anyone email you at this address other than me or this CC?"

"Just my friends, Sharon and Diane Brooke."

"All right. You can email them with the new address. Here, may I?"

He pulled up a chair next to mine, and we worked together to create a new account for me. Mr. Remington decided to set up the nanny account to forward automatically to his own. He thought it better not to let CC know that their emails were no longer getting through and for him to be able to monitor them in the event that he decided to take some action.

For the next quarter of an hour, we worked side by side. He wore an aftershave lotion with an intoxicating fragrance. A sense of contentment and almost joy nearly caused me to forget the fear the messages had instilled in me. I felt safe. I felt I could trust him.

And I was definitely looking forward to our trip to England together.

6

verything all right?" Mr. Remington leaned across the aisle of the Virgin Atlantic jet.

I nodded and tried to muster a smile. To be honest, I was fighting back my fears. Not only was this my first trip out of the country, but it was my first airplane trip ever. We had just taken off, and a loud *thunk* had startled me. I had looked around to see if anyone else was concerned about the sound, but no one else seemed to have heard it. The flight attendants were calmly going about their business. Mr. Remington must have noticed my anxiety.

"I just wondered what that loud noise was," I said.

"That's the landing gear being retracted," he explained. "You'll hear the same sound when we are getting ready to land and the wheels are lowered."

"Oh, of course." My smile was probably sheepish as Mr. Remington's held a hint of amusement.

I relaxed and settled back in my seat, turning my attention to Cadence, who was sitting next to the window. Ironically, she was much more a veteran traveler than I, and was happily watching a cartoon on her portable DVD player. The flight attendants began plying us with drinks. Mr. Remington recommended that I avoid caffeine and alcohol to lessen the effects of jet lag. I thanked him for his advice and ordered some ginger ale. I didn't remind him that I was too young to order alcohol anyway.

I was touched at how solicitous he had been. From the moment we had stepped foot in Dulles airport, he had taken it upon himself to explain everything and ensure that I was comfortable.

Comfortable indeed—especially in our first class seats. Midway through the flight, I stretched my legs by walking the length of the plane and back. After seeing how cramped the economy class seats were in comparison, I profusely thanked Mr. Remington for allowing me to fly up front with him and Cadence.

He had smiled graciously and said, "I wish I could claim an altruistic motive, but I frankly did not want to deal with a toddler on my own."

However, Cadence was far from being difficult. By the time I had finished my dinner of filet mignon, she had nodded off. I tucked her in, put away her DVD player, and turned on my own in-flight entertainment service to watch a movie.

Mr. Remington leaned over again, saying in a low voice,

"You may want to try the film on Channel 4. It's a romantic comedy that I think you'll like."

"Okay." I found the channel, adjusted my earphones, and pushed back my seat. As the opening credits ran, I caught the producer's name: Ethan Remington. I sat up in astonishment and excitedly reached across the aisle to grab his arm. "Mr. Remington! It's your film. I saw your name in the credits!"

He smiled, obviously pleased. "Yes. I hope you'll enjoy it. When it's over, let me know what you think."

I quieted my excitement over this discovery so that I could concentrate on the film and have an intelligent conversation with Mr. Remington at its conclusion. When the final credits rolled—and I again saw his name as the producer—we both removed our earphones and turned to each other.

"Well? How did you like it?" he asked.

"I loved it!" And I really had.

"Are you just saying that because I'm your boss and you have to?"

"Mr. Remington, you should know me better than that by now. I'm not the type to give false praise. No, I really loved it. Of course, most women do enjoy romance and happy endings. And I like British films and your British sense of humor. I really thought it was delightful. But I hadn't heard of it before. Has it done well?"

"It has done rather well in the UK, where it was released about two months ago. Now it's just making its way over the Atlantic, so we'll see how it's received in the States. And if it doesn't do well, there are always DVD sales and rentals. Jude Law tends to be a box office draw, though. Did you like him?"

"What's not to like? He's not only incredibly good-looking, but he was quite charming in that role."

"And what did you think of the leading lady?"

"She was very likable too, and the two of them had great chemistry."

"She's gorgeous, isn't she?" This was more of a statement than a question.

"Yes," I conceded. "She is. Who is she? I don't think I've seen her in anything before."

"Her name is Brittany Graham." He beamed. "I'm pleased to say that I discovered her."

"Really?" I tried to think of something to say. "That was a lucky find."

"Yes, yes, it was indeed. You'll be able to meet her, you know. She stars in another film we're releasing next week. It's a romantic drama set during the Battle of Britain. I'm having a party at Keswick Hall after the premier on Monday night, and she'll be there. I'd like you to come—"

"Mr. Remington," I interrupted. "I'm honored, but I couldn't possibly. I'm just the nanny."

"Precisely. I'd like Cadence there. I would like Brittany to meet her."

Thankfully, the plane cabin was dimly lit so that Mr. Remington could not see my burning cheeks.

"Of course." I hoped my tone sounded properly servile

and respectful. "Just let me know the time of the party and I'll have her ready."

I'm rather ashamed to admit that I no longer felt as positive about Miss Brittany Graham as I had while I was watching her in the movie. And I certainly did not look forward to meeting her.

"I think I'd better try to get some sleep," I said as I pushed the seat's reclining button and it slid out nearly flat—one more of the perks of first class. I tucked the blanket snuggly around Cadence and kissed her on the cheek. Then pulling my own blanket up to my chin, I whispered, "Good night, Mr. Remington."

"Good night, Jillian."

I may have been overly sensitive, but I was fairly certain that if I had glanced over at Mr. Remington, I would have seen him smiling.

❧

"Coffee or tea?" The flight attendant awakened me with breakfast.

Breakfast? Hadn't we just eaten dinner?

I looked at my watch. "But it's only one o'clock."

"It's actually six," Mr. Remington said. "You'll have less jet lag if you set your watch ahead and get yourself on UK time. Best you have some caffeine now."

"Tea, please," I responded as I put my seat upright.

"Coffee for me," he said. "Well, now, Jillian, did you enjoy your rest?"

"A little too brief. How do you deal with jet lag when you travel so often?"

"I don't believe in jet lag—for myself anyway. I just hit the ground running."

"I'm afraid I don't function well on a couple of hours' sleep. I'm glad Cadence is still asleep, but I don't know how I'll stay awake to take care of her today."

"Not to worry. We'll have some staff available at Keswick Hall to keep an eye on her until you have a chance to recover."

I smiled. "You think of everything, don't you?"

He returned my smile. "That's what I do."

"Mr. Remington, would you mind telling me a little about Keswick Hall? Is it as big a house as Carter Plantation?"

"Bigger. It's actually a castle, not a house."

"A castle? I've never even seen a real castle. Does it have a moat?"

"Of sorts. It was built on an island so it's surrounded by water. It's quite beautiful, really. And very old. It has a long hall that dates back to the time of Henry VIII. Several of his wives lived there from time to time."

"Did your family own it then?"

"No, it was a royal castle. Then Edward V gave it to the Fairfax family."

"Fairfax as in Fairfax County?"

"That's right. The same family who owned the half of Virginia that we Carters did not."

"But how did the castle end up in the Remingtons' possession?"

"My great-great-grandfather bought it in Queen Victoria's time."

"So your family is nobility?"

"No. Although that same great-great-grandfather did receive the knighthood for aiding Prince Albert in mounting the Great Exhibition at the Crystal Palace."

"But doesn't that make you a lord?"

"No, a knighthood is not a hereditary title."

"Oh." While I chewed on a Danish pastry, I mused on how little I knew about British customs and how little I really knew about Mr. Remington.

I ventured another question. "Mr. Remington, was your father an entrepreneur like you?"

"Not exactly. He inherited money and spent most of his time renovating the castle and opening it as a tourist destination."

"Was he young when he died?"

"I would say so, but then I'm over thirty. He was only fifty when he died of a heart attack. I was still at Oxford but had turned twenty-one so was old enough to inherit the estate."

"And your mother?"

He sighed. "My mother was also quite young—only fifty-five. Cancer. After my dad died, she decided to move back to Virginia to live, but she only survived him by seven years."

"I'm so sorry. It must be terrible to lose your parents—especially when they were so young. And then your wife—"

"Ah yes, my wife." Mr. Remington's face clouded. "I don't wish to speak of her."

"I'm sorry, sir. I didn't mean to upset you." I concentrated very hard on finishing my breakfast.

"Tell me, Jillian," Mr. Remington said after a long silence. "What do you know about my wife?"

Now I was perplexed. Hadn't he just said that he didn't wish to speak of her?

"To be honest, sir, very little," I responded respectfully. "All I know is that she . . . passed on."

I could not decipher the look on his face. Grief? Bitterness? Bewilderment?

"Yes," he said heavily. "She passed on . . ." He uttered a deep sigh, and it wrung my heart to hear it. "You see, Jillian, I have been abandoned by those I have loved." He added very quietly, "Sometimes I feel like even God himself has abandoned me."

"But, sir, that's not true. You still have Cadence, and your aunt, and all your friends." I wanted to add "and me" but caught myself. Instead I said, "You have lost your loved ones, but you have also been tremendously blessed. And God has not abandoned you."

He chuckled grimly. "Jillian, you are refreshingly earnest and innocent. I wish I were more like you, but sad to say, I am not. There's a lot about me that you don't know."

"Yes, but there is much that I do."

"Such as?"

"I'll admit that I don't know a lot of facts about you yet, like your favorite color, for instance, but I do know what you are like."

This evidently amused him. "Go on, what do you think I'm like?"

"Well, you are obviously well-educated and very intelligent, having gone to Oxford and Yale. You started your own company and have been amazingly successful, so you must be extremely hardworking and diligent, a visionary, a good planner with a gift for organization. You are dedicated to your family and care for those in your charge. You are a loving and affectionate father. You are considerate and generous. You—"

"That's enough, thank you, Jillian," Mr. Remington said, laughing. "You are very kind, but you haven't named any of my faults—of which there are many. So as I said: there is much about me that you don't know."

"I do know of some of your faults, but most people don't appreciate having their faults pointed out to them."

"Right you are. But for the sake of our discussion, let's see if you can name three of mine." He challenged me with his eyes. "Go on. Don't be afraid to be honest."

I took a deep breath. "If I had to name three of your faults, I would say that you have a quick temper, you are proud and arrogant, and you struggle with being self-absorbed."

"Ooh, touché." He seemed taken aback at my honesty. "You are quite observant, my little friend."

"I'm sorry if I've offended you."

"Not at all. I asked you to tell the truth, and I can see that you always do. That, young lady, is one of your finest qualities. Plus you evidently have a lot of courage." He paused. "It's aquamarine."

"Pardon?"

"My favorite color. It's aquamarine. Like the color of your bewitching eyes."

"Oh." To cover the blush that I knew had spread from my neck to my cheeks, I pulled out Cadence's sippy cup and signaled to a flight attendant.

"Excuse me, Miss. Could you please fill this with milk?"

"Yes, of course. Anything else? Should I take her tray?"

"No, thanks. She may want something to eat when she wakes up."

"Right. No problem." The flight attendant smiled and graciously took care of my request.

"Cadence certainly has been cooperative, hasn't she?" Mr. Remington observed with a touch of pride.

"Yes, she has. She's slept nearly the whole trip. I'm afraid you didn't really need me here in first class, after all."

"On the contrary, you have kept me quite entertained, Jillian. I've very much enjoyed our conversations. I hope we'll have some opportunities to talk again while we're at Keswick Hall. And I hope you'll enjoy your stay there with us."

From the way the trip had begun, I was sure that I would. But Mr. Remington was right. I knew so very little about him.

And I certainly had no idea what was in store for me at Keswick Hall.

7

*K*eswick Hall.

The very name can still conjure up in me—almost simultaneously—sensations of both delight and dread. My recollections of my first encounter with the place mostly evoke delight. Two days would elapse before the dread crept in.

Keswick Hall is ideally situated in Kent, the garden of England, midway between London and the coast of the English Channel. After a pleasant drive through the countryside from Gatwick airport, we passed through a private gate onto the estate. Mr. Remington explained that tour groups and visitors used the main entrance. We drove down a broad avenue bordered by dense groves of trees, which opened to the smooth lawn of a golf course. Suddenly the prospect of the castle rose before us, its heavy, honey-colored stones impossibly floating on a shimmering lake. Graceful swans—black as well as white—glided across the placid water.

I gasped involuntarily. "Oh my—it *is* beautiful!"

Mr. Remington smiled. "Yes," he agreed. "Some people deem Keswick the loveliest castle in all of Britain."

Our Bentley lumbered over the stone bridge of the gatehouse and along the circular drive of the castle's front lawn. Peacocks strolled about nonchalantly. Curious tourists stared at the arrival of a luxury car on the castle grounds. I realized that although we could see them, they couldn't see us through the tinted glass. We hustled through a side door into a private stairwell, where solicitous servants stood ready to greet us, collect our luggage, and transport it to our rooms.

A gray-haired matron, introduced as Nurse Poole, whisked Cadence from my arms while a pert and loquacious chambermaid named Karla showed me to my new quarters. Of medium height, with chin-length blond hair and blue eyes, Karla looked about my age and chatted comfortably with me as we climbed a dark oak spiral staircase. Through the casements of the Tudor-styled plaster and wood tower, I could see a fountain in the center of a stone courtyard.

"You're up here on the first floor, Miss. Right next to the nursery. The nursery used to be up on the second floor, but once Miss Cadence was born, Mr. Remington remodeled and moved it down next to his rooms."

"Didn't we come in on the first floor?" I asked in confusion.

"No, Miss. That was the ground floor. This is the first. The old nursery and some servants' rooms are up in the second floor garret. But for the most part the castle has only two floors, excepting the cellars, of course."

I was still puzzling over this apparent contradiction when Karla exclaimed, "Oh, that's right, you Americans call the ground level the first floor, don't you?"

I nodded.

"Why, you'll get used to our way of saying things, soon enough. Now the first floor, or second as you would say, is all private and not open to the tourists. But most of the castle on the ground level is open—during visiting hours, that is."

"And when are they?"

"Ten to four at this time of year, only we're having special evening candlelight Christmas tours this Thursday and Friday. After that, we'll close the castle for the winter months—except for the big premier party, of course. During the tourist season, we're closed on Sundays and Mondays. Mr. Remington gives all the staff Sundays off and then Monday is a big cleaning day for us."

At the top of the spiral staircase, a wooden statue of a soldier dressed like a cavalier stood guard on the newel post. His broad smile made him appear to be merrily laughing. I smiled back at him.

The landing of the back staircase opened to a large gallery brightened by windows overlooking the fountain court. Nearly opposite from us, the magnificent marble staircase of the central hall rose to the light-filled gallery. On our right, double doors opened to a sunny room painted in a warm pastel yellow with white trim. A white breakfast table and chairs sat in the bay window, with a view of the lake.

"This is the family dining room where Mr. Remington takes most of his meals," Karla said. "It has an electric dumbwaiter that goes down to the kitchen. His rooms are along this hallway running up to the front of the house."

We passed by a door that opened to a set of richly masculine rooms from which I could view the lake. My curiosity to see more than a glimpse of Mr. Remington's rooms would have to wait.

"And these," Karla said as we swept around the corner, "are the nursery rooms, here in the front of the New Castle, overlooking the lawn."

"*New* Castle?"

She shrugged. "Actually, this section is a lot newer than the original keep. The front part of the castle was built not 150 years ago by the present Mr. Remington's great-great-grandfather."

I thought that although "new," the crenellated building had been well constructed to blend harmoniously with the old. From the outside, one would never guess that this portion of the castle was over three hundred years younger than the rest.

I peeked into a comfortable and well-appointed nursery suite. The windows of the sitting room and play area projected over the central portico of the castle. I watched as Nurse Poole changed Cadence's diaper. Giving me a curt nod, the elderly woman said, "Don't worry about the baby,

Miss. I'll take good care of her today while you get your rest. Mr. Ethan's orders."

"Thank you, Mrs. Poole. If you have any questions though, please ask."

"We'll be fine. I've taken care of Miss Cadence many times before, and even Mr. Ethan himself back in the day."

She did seem, if not a Mary Poppins type, at least experienced and competent. I relaxed to think that Mr. Remington had provided his own infant nurse to spell me.

"Thank you," I repeated. "I am really tired."

I followed Karla to the next door. "This is your room, and your bags are already here," she said. "Your bathroom and toilet are there just across the hall."

We stepped into a small but cheerfully decorated chamber. Although Keswick Hall was beautiful and romantic beyond anything I could imagine, my room fell somewhat below the contemporary comforts of Carter Plantation. Other than a washbasin, an electric hot-water pot with a coffee and tea tray, a small television, baby monitor, and a telephone, there were no other modern amenities. But I did not complain. Surely, I—who had bounced from one foster home to another— could not. No matter how modest my accommodations, I was absolutely thrilled to be staying in an English castle— especially down the corridor from Mr. Remington.

Karla pointed to a door in the wall. "That connects to the nursery. It looks like oak, but it's a metal fire door underneath. Mr. Remington had fire doors installed throughout the castle after the big fire at Windsor Castle."

"It's a *tromp d'oeile*. How clever," I said.

"A what?"

"Trick of the eye."

"Right. Well, now, if you need anything or have any questions," Karla said, "you can pick up your phone and dial one for the butler, two for the housekeeper, and three for the kitchen. Oh, and zed is for the porter or security guard at the gatehouse. If you want to dial out of the castle, you dial nine first and then the number. But the switchboard closes for incoming calls after five, except for Mr. Remington's private line. The phones come back on at seven in the morning."

My head ached and I rubbed my temples. "I'm sorry, Karla, but I'm not sure I'll remember all this."

"Not to worry. The numbers are written on the phone. And on the back of your door is a floor plan to the castle. It shows the exits in case of fire, but it will help you find your way around too. Maybe after you've had a chance to wash up and take a nap, you might want to go down to the gatehouse and tag along on an official guided tour, just to get oriented. Otherwise, I'll try to show you around when I get off work at five."

"Thanks. That's nice of you. But where is your room?"

"Oh, I don't live here. I have a flat in Maidstone. Since Mr. Remington doesn't stay here all the time, only the housekeeper and the butler, Mr. and Mrs. Brown, actually live in the castle. The rest of us just work our shifts and go home."

"It must be pretty quiet around here at night," I observed.

"Must be—except when the house is opened over the holidays for candlelight tours or the times Mr. Remington has parties."

"With so few people living in this huge place, do you think it's safe?" I asked, thinking of those threatening emails from CC.

"Safe? To be sure, Miss. It's a castle now, isn't it? It's not like anyone can break in. Plus there's a security guard at the gatehouse 24/7."

She walked over to the dresser and picked up a name badge attached to a lanyard. "Wear this during tourist hours. It's your passport to the private sections of the castle. I'd attach your room key to it too. Mr. Remington is very careful about security. Still, you should always lock your door. Leastways, I think every woman has to be careful, don't you? Security guards or not. With all the tourists about during the day, it doesn't hurt to take precautions."

She added, "But if it's ghosts you're worried about, you needn't be. There have never been any reports of hauntings around here. No, I think you're perfectly safe here."

"I'm glad to hear it. By the way, do you spell your name with a K or a C?"

"With a K."

I sighed with relief. "That's good."

"Sorry?"

I recovered myself to respond, "It's good to know—so I'll spell it correctly."

"It's funny you should ask. My mother spelled it with a C, but I changed it to K. I think it looks better. Stronger somehow. Don't you think so?"

"Yes, very nice. Thanks so much, Karla. You've been very helpful."

"Sure thing," she said, stepping back into the hallway. "By the way, if you get hungry, you can just find your way down to the kitchen and help yourself. Just go back down the hall to the staircase with the statue of the Laughing Cavalier and go down to the basement. The kitchen is right there. You can't miss it. Staff breakfast is served between half past six and eight, and lunch is from half past eleven to one in the staff dining room next to the kitchen. Check with Mrs. Brown to see if there are any cooked dinners scheduled."

"Okay. Thanks again, Karla."

I closed the door behind her and bolted it. After setting the alarm clock for noon, I folded back the bedspread, flopped down on the bed, and fell promptly to sleep.

⚜

The alarm woke me from a deep slumber. It took me a few minutes to remember where I was. I was so tempted to roll over and go back to sleep for the rest of the day when I remembered Mr. Remington's advice to take a short nap and then get up and proceed with the day, going to bed on British time so that my body would quickly acclimate.

I washed my face, brushed my teeth, changed into jeans

and a sweater, and pulled my hair up into a ponytail. Locking my door and placing the lanyard around my neck, I found my way down the hall, past the laughing statue and down the oak spiral staircase to the staff dining room.

I glanced around the room and was surprised to see several tables filled with workers, many wearing uniforms identifying them as chambermaids, gardeners, or cooks. The attendant at the bountiful buffet table read my badge and motioned me to an empty table, but Karla spied me and waved me over to join her.

"You can sit here with me, if you don't mind," she said.

"Why should I mind?" I asked, slipping into an empty chair across from her. "I'd rather not eat alone. Why did the waiter want me to sit over there by myself?"

"As the nanny you have a particular position. You are in a station above the rest of us, so should eat separately or with the Browns, our butler and housekeeper. But they usually take their meals in their own quarters."

"Why would I want to eat alone? I don't understand."

"That's because you're American. Believe it or not, we still have a class structure over here, especially in a great house such as this."

"That seems pretty silly in this day and age. Back home, Mr. Remington doesn't observe such conventions. I was invited to have dinner with him and his aunt every evening."

"You see, as the nanny you are in a unique class of your own here—not quite a servant nor obviously on a level with the lord of the manor. I agree it's rather silly, but that's just the way it's done. If I were you, I wouldn't expect to see much of Mr. Remington while you are here."

I tried to swallow my disappointment along with my meal. Yet, I reasoned, Mr. Remington would not neglect spending time with Cadence. I would doubtless see him more often than Karla supposed.

As it turned out, that evening I literally ran into him.

8

After lunch I had taken Karla's advice and, with camera in tow, joined one of the official tour groups of the castle. I was amazed at the expansive banqueting hall of Henry VIII and the queen's gallery, both lined with windows overlooking the lake; and I was awestruck to think that I was lucky enough to be actually residing in a place of such antiquity, history, and beauty.

After the tour, I changed into a warm-up suit and training shoes. Jogging over the bridge, I took off on a run through the park surrounding the castle. The sun set much earlier than I expected. I watched from across the lake as it dipped behind the trees, its dying rays spilling liquid honey across the castle stones and into the golden circlet of water.

The sight pierced me with a poignant longing. It was then, captivated by the scene, I nearly ran into Mr. Remington.

He grabbed me by the arms to keep us both from stumbling. "Steady, there! My word, Jillian, you are like an elf appearing out of nowhere."

"Mr. Remington! I'm so sorry! I didn't see you. I was watching the sunset. Isn't it amazing? I wish I had my camera."

"I'm glad you happened to be here," he replied. "I try to get to this spot as often as I can to see it. Stay with me a moment and watch."

We stood gazing in comfortable silence as the Creator brushed new strokes on the sky's canvas in a constantly changing artistic display. As the dusk gathered around us, so did a chill. I clasped my arms tightly against my chest and shivered.

Mr. Remington noted it. "You're cold. Allow me." Before I could even think to object, he had removed his leather jacket and placed it over my shoulders. "May I walk you back?"

"Thank you, but you don't need to. I'll be fine."

"I know I don't need to, Jillian, but I would like to. I'm heading back myself, and besides"—he smiled—"you now have my jacket."

I hoped in the growing shadows that he could not see the blush I could feel creeping up my neck and into my cheeks. I tried to keep my voice steady and nonchalant. "Then, of course, you may."

We began walking along the perimeter of the lake toward the gatehouse.

"So, Jillian, what have you been doing with your free time today?"

"I took a short nap as you suggested, ate some lunch, and joined a guided tour of the castle."

"You've been busy then. And what did you learn on your tour?"

"That there's much more to learn. There's so much to see here, and maybe it's because of the jet lag, but I just couldn't take it all in. I'm tempted to bring Cadence with me on another tour tomorrow."

"I'll tell you what. Why don't I take you both on a private tour tomorrow afternoon?"

I hadn't expected this. "But your work, surely—"

"Listen, I had appointments all afternoon, and tomorrow morning I have an estate staff meeting and conference calls. But after lunch, I'll be free and eager not to have to work. In fact, I'd like you and Cadence to have lunch with me in the family dining room at half past twelve. Then we'll try to fit in a tour before her naptime. Perhaps we should take advantage of this fine weather we're having and do a complete grounds tour. Then later when it's wet out, we can tour the castle."

"That sounds great."

"Excellent." We walked over the stone bridge, past the gatehouse, and he nodded at the security guard. "Good evening, Doug."

"Evening, Mr. Remington."

"All quiet?"

"Yes, sir. The last of the tourists are gone. It's all yours now. Mrs. Poole is with the baby, and the Browns are snug in their flat."

"Right. Thanks. By the way, Doug, this is our new nanny, Miss Jillian Dare. Jillian, our night porter and head security guard, Doug Crooke."

Mr. Crooke's alert hazel eyes peered at me through silver-rimmed glasses. I confidently returned his gaze, judging him to be in his early forties and well over six feet tall, with a muscular but slim build. As he shoved up his cap in a polite salute, I noticed his brown hair ringed a bald pate. I must have passed his scrutiny because he extended his hand in welcome. "How do you do, Miss? I saw you out jogging and figured you to be the new one."

I was surprised that I had not managed to escape un-noticed. "I'm fine, thanks," I said as I shook his hand. "Nice to meet you."

"I hope you enjoy your stay at our fair castle. We'll do our part to keep you safe and sound. Have a nice evening, Miss. Sir." His attention returned to the bank of surveillance monitors.

"Thank you," I said sincerely.

The castle lawn and circular drive were well lit. All was quiet. And I did feel secure, indeed.

"Are you hungry?" Mr. Remington asked as he slid a key card into the lock of the side entrance.

"Why, yes, I am. Although I'm not sure what meal I should be eating now." I glanced at my watch. Five o'clock. I felt like it should be bedtime.

"Tea or supper, whichever you please," Mr. Remington said, letting me pass before him into the private foyer and shutting and bolting the door behind us. "Here, let me take that jacket." He lifted it from my shoulders and hung it on one of the hooks lining the walls. "Come down to the kitchen with me and we'll see what we can scrounge up. I didn't think we'd be up to a full dinner, so I let Cook have the evening off."

I followed him down the stairwell to the basement, where low lights had been left on. Mr. Remington strode to the commercial-size stainless steel refrigerators and rummaged around for a few minutes.

"What do you fancy?" he asked. "We have lunch leftovers, or I could cook up some omelets for us."

"An omelet sounds fabulous. Would you like me to make it?"

His expression was mockingly crestfallen. "Come now, Jillian. You don't believe I can cook?"

"Umm . . . we've always had our meals prepared by someone else, so I really wouldn't know."

He motioned to a stool by the counter. "Sit here. Watch and be amazed."

I scooted up on the stool while he poked his head back into the refrigerator.

"What would you like in your omelet?" he asked from its depths. "Cheese? Green pepper? Mushrooms? Scallions? Ham?"

"Cheese and mushrooms, please," I answered.

He pulled out eggs, cheese, mushrooms, and green peppers and ham for himself, piling them on the counter. Then after disappearing into a pantry for a few minutes, he emerged with a wine bottle and two glasses.

"Rosé?" He began pouring before I responded.

"No, thank you. I'm not old enough to drink, remember?"

He stopped pouring and looked at me. "No, I had forgotten. How old are you again?"

"Twenty."

"Twenty," he repeated softly. "So young. I can't believe it. Those eyes of yours make you seem much older."

"What do you mean?"

"I mean, when I look into your eyes, I see wisdom and maturity far beyond a mere twenty years."

He continued filling one glass and then poured a small amount in the other. "Well, now, the legal age for drinking in the UK is eighteen, not twenty-one, so technically you are old enough to imbibe here. Don't worry; I won't attempt to corrupt you. But if you would humor me with just a taste, it would please me. The wine is made right here on our estate."

He held up the bottle for me to read the label, Keswick Hall. "There have been vineyards here dating back to at least 1086 when they were recorded in the Domesday Book, so it's an ancient and esteemed label. Would you like to try a bit?"

I felt it would be rude to refuse him. "Sure. Just a sip, though."

He showed me how to swirl the wine in the glass, sniff

it, take a sip, hold it in my mouth, swish it around to savor the flavor, and only then swallow. Then he watched me expectantly. I felt a strange sense of satisfaction that my first introduction to wine tasting would be under the tutelage of Mr. Remington. The wine had a sweet, fruity taste. I nodded my approval.

"It's good."

He smiled. "Now what else would you like to drink? A glass of milk or a cup of tea?"

"Tea, please, but I'll make it." I hopped down from my stool and fixed a pot of tea while he returned to the task of making the omelets, sipping from his wineglass as he chopped, sautéed, and cooked. He served up the omelets with a flourish and sat across from me at the counter.

I bowed my head to give thanks silently and picked up my fork.

"You may say grace out loud for us both," he said. "I might not seem like much of a Christian, but if you remember, I do give thanks for my blessings."

"Of course." I bowed my head again. "Thank you, Lord, for this food and bless the hands that prepared it. And bless our conversation. Amen."

"Amen." He held up his wineglass. "And cheers."

"Cheers." I smiled and cut into the omelet. For the second time I nodded my approval. "Hmm—this is really good."

"Thank you. I am vindicated." He dug in, and his omelet quickly vanished. He poured himself a second glass of wine.

His eyes shone brightly. He seemed in an unusually happy mood, although I suspected that the wine had something to do with that.

"Jillian," he said, "thank you for sharing supper with me tonight. I do despise eating alone, and I find you to be delightful company."

"Thank you. And thanks for making such a delicious omelet."

He bowed his head in acknowledgment. "You are most welcome. Now, although I dislike bringing up business after hours, would you mind if I run over the week's schedule with you?"

"Of course not," I said, but I did mind just a little to be reminded that I was in Mr. Remington's employ. He had such an easy, natural manner with me that, for a few minutes, I had forgotten.

"Right. Now then, tomorrow morning at eight, after what I hope is sufficient time to recover from the trip, you will be back on duty with Cadence. We will have lunch at half past twelve and the private tour as discussed. You will have your afternoons free as you did at home, while Nurse Poole watches the baby. I have an engagement in town tomorrow night and will need you to stay with Cadence then.

"On Thursday and Friday evenings, the castle will be open from seven to nine for the candlelight Christmas tours. You are welcome to take Cadence along on one if you wish. We'll have madrigal singers and hot cider and refreshments served in the Henry VIII banqueting hall, a stringed quartet in the drawing room, and carolers in the entrance hall. It's quite a lovely event, and I think you will enjoy it.

"Then on Monday night, we'll have our big premier party. Brittany Graham and others in the cast and crew will be staying overnight. Which reminds me. Calvin will be arriving on Thursday as well."

"Mr. Cole?"

"Yes. I wanted him to attend the premier. Plus we have a private matter to discuss with my solicitors here."

"I'm sure you'll be glad to have his company."

"Yes. Although right now I'm enjoying yours, but I can tell by that disconcerting look on your face that I have ruined our conversation by bringing up business."

I was considering the unpleasantness of sharing the house and Mr. Remington's attention with the glamorous Brittany Graham, but I couldn't admit to that.

"I was just thinking about how awkward I am in such society. It would probably be better if I didn't attend the premier party."

"Nonsense. I've already told you that I would like to show off Cadence. You might even find you'll enjoy meeting some film stars. At any rate, Cadence goes to bed fairly early so you may excuse yourself then if you like. But I'd like her at the party by eight."

"Yes, sir."

He sighed. "I do wish you wouldn't call me 'sir.' It makes me feel like such an old man."

He shoved his plate aside and took another sip of wine.

"Now, then, Jillian, tell me how you plan to spend your free time while you are here."

"Well, back home, I like to run in my free time or take pictures or read. So I suppose I will do those things too—unless I have an opportunity to do some sightseeing."

He stood up abruptly. "That reminds me! Wait here just a minute. I have something for you. Just sit here while I get it. I'll be right back."

I overcame my astonishment enough to collect the dishes and rinse them in the sink while he was absent. I was putting the food back in the refrigerator when he returned carrying a Christmas gift bag.

"I know it's a bit early," he said, "but I figured you could use it now. No need to wait. Merry Christmas, Jillian." He held the bag out to me.

Stunned, I stared at him.

"Go on," he urged. "Take it. It won't bite."

"But, Mr. Remington, you shouldn't have."

"Just open it."

I took the bag and, setting it on the counter, reached in and pulled out a small box wrapped in tissue paper. Unwinding the paper, I uncovered a camera box. A digital camera! And so tiny it could fit in my hand.

"I thought it would be nice for you to have now so that you can take pictures while you sightsee," he said eagerly. "Plus it's little enough that it can fit in your pocket. So you can take it with you when you go running, should you chance to see another sunset over the lake."

"Mr. Remington, I don't know what to say."

He grinned. "'Thank you' is customary, I believe."

"Thank you. Very much. I'm just overwhelmed by your thoughtfulness and generosity." I forced myself to look him in the eye. "Really. Thank you. I don't know how I'll ever repay you."

"You're quite welcome. And you needn't think about repaying me. It wouldn't be a gift if I expected something in return. It makes me happy to be able to give you something you need, and that is return enough. I will, however, expect to see some very fine pictures."

"I'll have to study the direction manual first and figure out how to use it."

"It's not difficult. I'd be happy to help you with it tomorrow, and later, I'll show you how to download the pictures on the computer."

I shook my head. "Why are you so nice to me?"

He smiled. "It's my pleasure. I must confess to you, Jillian, that since the first day we met—the day you pulled me out of my wrecked car—I have thought that you would be good for me. You've certainly been marvelous with Cadence, and I am most grateful for that. So consider this a token of my appreciation.

"Now," he said, rising from his stool, "I'm sure you must be tired and ready for bed. I'll walk you up to your room."

He switched off the lights except for the fluorescent ones over the sink and stove areas, and followed me up the stairs. We both checked in on Cadence, who was sleeping soundly in her crib. Nurse Poole had left the monitor on and had retired to her third—or second—floor bedroom.

After bending down and kissing Cadence, Mr. Remington saw me safely to my room.

"I'm just down the hall if you need me," he said. "And my study also connects to the nursery on the other side."

"Thank you, Mr. Remington. For the camera, for supper, for trusting me with your daughter, for everything."

"Thank you for keeping me company tonight. I enjoy our conversations and times together and am looking forward to tomorrow. Good night, Jillian."

"Good night, Mr. Remington." I closed my door and leaned my head against it.

I was looking forward to tomorrow too.

9

The next day I found Mr. Remington staring out the window of the family dining room, a scowl clouding his face. He brightened, though, when I walked in carrying Cadence.

"Ah, here you are!" Rising hastily, he took Cadence from my arms and secured her in her high chair. He kissed her chubby cheek and then withdrew a chair for me across the table from his. "There you go, Jillian. I'm so glad to see you lovely girls. All these business meetings grow quite tiresome."

"Has it been a difficult day for you?" I asked.

"In some respects," he said grimly. "But let's not talk business. I would like to forget all that for now. It's such a bore. Please, say your grace and help yourself to lunch."

Hot soup and sandwiches had been placed on the table. I

bowed my head to give thanks and, after serving Cadence, began eating.

Mr. Remington looked up from his soup and forced a smile. "All right, I'm in the mood for some nonbusiness conversation, so talk to me," he commanded.

I sat in silence.

"Talk to me," he repeated. "Don't you have anything to say?"

I shook my head.

He scrutinized me. "Hmm . . . you seem annoyed."

"I'm sorry, sir. I'd be happy to talk to you if I knew what topics interested you. I'm not one to talk randomly just for the sake of talking. It's rather difficult to strike up a conversation when you don't know what subject is of common interest. Perhaps you could ask me some questions about what interests you."

"Good point. Rather rude of me, I suppose, to command you to speak as though you were a dog. I beg your pardon. Tell me then, Jillian, do you enjoy taking care of Cadence? Are you happy?"

"Very much. She's a delightful little girl. And yes, I'm quite happy."

"Why are you smiling that enigmatic smile?"

"I was just thinking about how few employers seem to care much about the happiness of their nannies."

"Ah yes. I do pay you, don't I? It's easy for me to forget that, although I'm sure you do not. Do you feel well-compensated? Well-treated?"

"Absolutely. You've been more than generous."

"Good. How do you like England so far?"

"I love it. I've been an Anglophile for as long as I can remember, so I'm thrilled to be here."

"Excellent. And what is it that you've admired about England?"

"I find the history of the country fascinating. All the kings and queens and their stories are so interesting to me. And I love the literature. I'm not a big fan of American lit—except maybe some contemporary authors."

"But you didn't go to university. So all this history and literature has been self-taught?"

"For the most part. I love to read."

He shoved his plate aside. "Are you finished? I have something to show you."

I quickly swallowed my last bites and wiped Cadence's face and hands. Mr. Remington took her from the high chair and swung her up on his shoulder.

"Come with me," he said.

He strode off down the hallway and I scurried to keep up with him. We passed the row of windows overlooking the fountain court and the open marble staircase to the foyer below, where a tour group had gathered to listen to a docent reciting the history of the castle.

We passed several doors to opulently furnished boudoirs. He slowed to allow me a glimpse as we walked by.

"These are our guest rooms," he said. "Brittany Graham will stay in this corner room, which has a view of the fountain on one side and the lake on the other. And this one"—he indicated a more masculine room with dark mahogany furniture and framed prints of horses—"is where Calvin stays. We also have more guest rooms up on the second floor. And then there are the rooms in the old section of the castle, but those are on display to the public and rarely used anymore."

"And Mrs. Poole stays upstairs, doesn't she?"

"Yes, she stays here at the castle when we are in town. The old nursery was up there, but I moved it next to my room when Cadence was born." He slid back a double pocket door to a large parlor occupying the front corner of the house.

"Now then, this is our private family drawing room," he said. "It's right next door to yours, so you are welcome to make yourself at home here—read, study, relax—whatever you please."

The room was comfortably furnished with overstuffed sofas, ottomans, and reading chairs. A marble fireplace graced the far wall.

"Thanks, this is really nice."

"I'll show you a little secret that I think you'll enjoy." Walking over to the far outside corner of the room, he opened what appeared to be a closet door. "Follow me."

I did and found myself in a narrow spiral staircase. At the bottom, we stepped into the vast library of the castle.

"Oh my gosh," I exclaimed. "A secret staircase! That is so cool."

His eyes sparkled. "I thought you'd like that. So you see, if you're bored at night, you can sneak down to the library and grab any book you like. The staircase is built into the turret. There's another one on the opposite side of the house, which connects from my study to the conference room below. I love suddenly appearing at a boardroom meeting like a phantom out of nowhere."

He chuckled. "It's quite fun to see the surprise on those dour faces. Now, let's get out of here before the tour catches up with us."

He opened the door to the staircase and allowed me to climb the stairs ahead of him.

"The weather is holding," he said. "So, would you care to see more of the park?"

"Yes, that would be great."

"All right. Get Cadence changed and suited up and meet me in the family foyer in fifteen minutes. Bring a jacket for yourself and don't forget your camera."

"Yes, sir." I swiftly followed his instructions and waited for him with Cadence in her stroller a few minutes before the allotted time.

He smiled as he entered the foyer. "Ah, good. You are prompt. Did you bring your new camera?"

"Yes, I did," I answered, holding it up for him to see.

"Have you figured out how it works yet?"

"A little, but I haven't had time to read the directions manual."

"May I?" he asked, extending his hand. I placed the camera in the wide palm of his large hand. "Let me give you some quick pointers, and then you can have fun playing around with it."

He proceeded to explain some basics of the camera's functions. We stood very close together, our heads nearly touching, our fingers brushing against each other. The scent of his cologne and his near presence intoxicated me. I could scarcely breathe.

"Do you think you can manage?" he asked, looking down at me.

I caught his eye and then glanced away. "Yes. Thank you."

"Right. Well, just experiment and we'll try to download the pictures on the computer later tonight." He stopped himself. "Oh, sorry, not tonight. I have the film publicity party in town. Perhaps tomorrow then. But let's get going. There's much to see, and we don't want Cadence to miss her naptime."

He leaned over to release her from the stroller. "This pushchair's a bit awkward on the pebbled pathways so I'll carry her."

He led the way to a rose garden, which lay mostly dormant, although a few stalwart bushes still bravely bloomed. I reflected how beautiful and fragrant it must be in the summer months. With Cadence perched wide-eyed on Mr. Remington's shoulder, we strolled together among hedges and past flower beds and fountains.

He talked easily about the variety of flowers in the gardens and his interest in horticulture, and then about the history of Keswick Hall and all his father, grandfather, and great-grandfather had done to renovate and improve the property. He clearly loved his ancestral home and enjoyed speaking about it.

As for me, I thoroughly enjoyed listening to him.

We wandered down to the gatehouse, where Mr. Remington secured a golf cart with a baby's car seat already installed. I buckled in Cadence and then had the freedom to snap pictures as Mr. Remington drove slowly around the estate park. He talked as he drove and I eagerly listened.

Suddenly he stopped self-consciously. "I hope I'm not boring you, Jillian."

"Not at all. I'm learning a lot."

"You're a good listener, you know."

"I like to listen to you."

He smiled. "Since you have so much wisdom for someone so young, let me ask you something. I know a young man—well, perhaps not so young to you—who several years ago made a terrible mistake. He didn't do anything morally wrong—just had a very bad lapse in judgment."

He stared into the distance for a few minutes, reflecting.

"That lapse or error or mistake, or whatever you'd call it," he continued, "has had dreadful repercussions in his life. For a while, he tried to forget his sorrows by indulging in the fast and loose lifestyle of the rich and famous, but all he found there was emptiness. The sorrows only compounded not lessened."

He turned to me. "What would you advise such a man?

Is he doomed to a life of unhappiness because of one bad choice, or is there hope for him?"

"There is always hope," I said quietly, knowing full well he was speaking of himself.

"But in what? Riches have not provided solace, and people have only disappointed him."

"Surely, he can hope in God."

"God," he scoffed, "didn't protect him from making that capital error in judgment. God has abandoned him to a life of remorse and regret."

"I'm quite sure God has not abandoned him. And he can't blame God for a choice he made of his own free will. He only needs to turn back to God and ask his help. After all, the best cure for regret is repentance."

"Repentance from what, though? He didn't do anything wrong. He is being punished for a mistake."

"But you said that since his mistake, he has turned away from God and has done things that he regrets. Therefore, perhaps he should repent of them."

"That's true. Do you think that God would receive him back again?"

"Of course. Remember the parable of the prodigal son? The father welcomed him with open arms and had a feast for him."

"Right. But I think that mere repentance is not enough. I think that what is wanted—what is needed—is a total reformation."

"I'm sure you're right about that."

"Could someone like you help this wretched man make this reformation in his life?"

"I would be happy to try."

He observed me very closely. "I believe you would, Jillian. I believe you would."

❧

My afternoon with Mr. Remington had been absolutely delightful. I seldom had enjoyed another person's company so much in my entire life. I'll confess that I experienced some pangs of regret when he left for London to attend the publicity party for his new film. I knew he would be out late and I would not see him again until morning.

After bathing Cadence, giving her a bottle, and rocking and singing her to sleep, I crept down the spiral staircase to the library. What a wonderland where I could lose myself! I spent over an hour perusing the shelves and finally selected *Rebecca* by Daphne du Maurier. I had just settled myself in a comfy chair in the family room when I heard the phone ringing.

Karla had informed me that the castle phone lines were shut down after five, except for Mr. Remington's private line. He had left his cordless phone in the nursery sitting room in case I needed to call him. But I was quite surprised to hear it ringing, and hurried down the hallway to answer it.

The ringing had stopped by the time I reached the phone. I checked on Cadence, who was sleeping undisturbed, and decided to read in the sitting room where I could keep an eye on her as well as answer the phone.

A few minutes later, it rang again. I quickly picked it up.

"Hello? Jillian Dare speaking."

Silence greeted me.

"Hello? Mr. Remington?"

Silence.

"Hello?"

Silence.

"Hello?"

Silence.

"Helloooo. Anybody there?"

Silence.

I hung up. *That was strange.*

I had just sat back down and opened my book when the phone rang again.

I quickly picked it up. "Hello? Mr. Remington? I'm sorry, but you must have been cut off. Is everything all right?"

Silence.

"Mr. Remington? . . . Hello?"

Silence.

I hung up. Minutes later the phone rang again. I was beginning to feel frightened. I took a deep breath and picked up the phone.

"Hello?"

Silence.

"Who is this?" I demanded.

Silence.

I hung up. Before it could ring again, I dialed Mr. Remington's cell phone number.

"Hello?" he answered. He had to shout over the buzz of conversations and the booming bass of a rock band. "Jillian, is that you? Is anything wrong?"

"I'm sorry to bother you, sir, but did you just call?"

"No. Why?"

"Someone called several times, but when I answered there was no one there, or there was someone there but they didn't say anything."

"Sorry, did you just say that someone has called my private line but they aren't identifying themselves?"

"They aren't saying anything. I thought I should check with you to see if you were trying to get through but had been cut off."

"No, it wasn't me." He paused, then asked, "Is Cadence all right?"

"Yes, she's fine. She's asleep in the next room."

"Good. Well, it was probably some sort of prankster."

"But what prankster would have your unlisted number?"

"Jillian, are you all right?"

"I'm fine. Just a little creeped out."

"Tell you what. This party is winding down, so I'll come home now. Don't answer the phone anymore. Just let it ring if you like."

"But what if you need to call?"

"Right. Okay, let's have a signal. If I need to call, I'll ring once and then hang up. That will be your signal that it's me. Then I'll call back and you can pick up. All right?"

"Okay."

"All right, don't worry. I'll be home soon."

"Thanks, Mr. Remington."

"Right. I'll see you soon. Bye."

I hung up, and not two minutes later, the phone rang again. It rang and rang and rang and rang. I thought I would scream. A few minutes later, it rang again and again and again. A third time, it rang and rang and rang and rang. I sat frozen, praying it would stop. Praying that Mr. Remington would come home soon.

Finally, the caller gave up. The silence threatened me. I turned on the radio to a classical station and I checked that all the doors to the hallway were locked.

Then I sat and waited for Mr. Remington.

10

I must have dozed off when the phone rang again. I awoke with a start. One ring. I held my breath. A few seconds' pause. The phone rang again. I answered it.

"Hello?"

"Jillian, it's me." Mr. Remington's deep voice reassured me. "I'm just coming up the stairs now and didn't want to frighten you. I'll be at the door in less than a minute."

"Yes, sir. Thank you." Opening the nursery door, I looked expectantly down the hallway and felt a flood of relief seeing his powerful figure striding toward me.

He clasped my arms and studied my face with concern. "You are frightened, aren't you? It's probably just some prankster who randomly dialed my number, having a bit of fun at your expense."

"It wasn't funny, sir. It was creepy. Do you think it could be CC?"

"CC?"

"Remember the threatening emails?"

"Ah yes."

"Do you think it could be the same person who is calling?"

"I . . . doubt it."

But I am certain I saw concern flash across his eyes. "How is Cadence?" he asked, stepping into the nursery and rushing over to her crib.

She snored blissfully unaware, sprawled on her back. He bent over and kissed her gently on the cheek.

Ushering me back into the sitting room, he motioned for me to be seated.

"Do you have any idea who CC is?" I asked.

"Don't worry. I have someone making discreet inquiries."

"And the caller?"

"I'll contact the phone company in the morning and have a tracer put on the line. If they call again—which I doubt— we'll be able to track them."

"Don't you have caller ID?"

"Ironically, that phone is on the old landline. It's not a RemTel phone and so, no, I don't have caller ID. Explain again. Did the caller say anything or make any sound?"

"No. All I could hear was their breathing."

"Heavy breathing?"

"No. Almost no sound at all. Just this creepy silence."

"I'm so sorry that you were frightened. I'm here now and will deal with any other calls. We'll sort this out in the morning. Meanwhile, it's late and you need your sleep. Don't worry. The castle is quite secure and no one will bother you."

"Okay. Thanks for coming home, Mr. Remington." I rose. "How did your party go?"

"Brilliant. Thanks for asking. Brittany looked stunning and the photographers were out in full force, so all bodes well for a spectacular premier and plenty of publicity."

"I'm so glad," I said, swallowing my envy of the "stunning" Brittany. "Well, good night."

"Good night, Jillian," he said gently. "Sleep tight."

I didn't see much of Mr. Remington the next day. In the morning he seemed preoccupied with meetings and plans for the premier party. Calvin Cole arrived in the afternoon. I chanced to see him as he settled in his guest room. He greeted me in a friendly manner and made much over Cadence. He and Mr. Remington went out to play some holes of golf on the estate course, and in the evening, they made a trip into London to have dinner with friends and, I presumed, Miss Brittany Graham.

The first of the Christmas candlelight tours was held that night to the wonderful anticipation of both guests and staff. Festive garlands and floral arrangements graced the castle, and candelabras illumined the public rooms with a warm glow. Minstrels and madrigals greeted guests with harmonious carols, and a stringed quartet enchanted everyone in the splendid drawing room. Refreshments of hot mulled cider and enticing sweets beckoned in the Henry VIII banqueting hall.

I completely enjoyed wandering among the ornate rooms, sampling the wares, and mingling with the guests while listening to the music. I had placed Cadence facing forward in a Snugli so that I could more easily carry her about. Thankfully, her petite size kept her from tiring my back or shoulders. She also delighted in the sights and sounds of the season, and many of the guests smiled indulgently at her as she clapped her tiny hands or babbled in excitement.

One guest, however, made me uneasy as she hovered about on the fringes of the crowd. She was tall and slender and dressed entirely in white, with a shawl shrouding her face. Long, gloved fingers drew the shawl tightly. At first glance, I wondered if the shawl were a burqua or some other religious veil, but when I noted the style of her dress, I doubted that conjecture. Her full-length gown evoked the Victorian era and reminded me of posters I had seen in the airport advertising Sir Andrew Lloyd Webber's musical *The Woman in White*. I had noticed them because Wilkie Collins's eponymous gothic novel was one of my favorites.

The woman did not speak to anyone and glided soundlessly—almost ghostlike—from room to room. I had the uncomfortable sense that she was following us. In the library, she suddenly disappeared, and I felt relief that she had left the tour.

As the guests began to disperse, I carried Cadence up to the nursery by way of the private spiral staircase to the landing with the Laughing Cavalier. I changed her and dressed her for bed in a soft fleece sleeper. After warming some milk, I settled in a rocking chair and sang to her as she drank from her bottle contentedly, twisting a tendril of my hair between her fingers. I gave in to the luxury of the peaceful moment and closed my eyes as we rocked together in harmony.

After some time, we heard the nursery door creak open. I hadn't locked it. Cadence sat up suddenly, our peace broken. My heart froze at the white apparition standing in the doorway.

A ghost!

Then I collected myself.

I recognized the mysterious woman in white. She said nothing, merely stood with the shawl covering her face, staring at us.

"M-m-may I help you?" I stammered.

She did not speak.

"I'm sorry," I said, "but these are private rooms and not part of the tour. You'll have to go back to the marble staircase and down to the entrance hall."

She stood silently a moment longer and then glided away. I rose and followed her to make sure that she did not try to trespass anywhere else. I watched as she descended the stairs, and then, returning quickly to the nursery, I put Cadence to bed and bolted the hallway doors before retiring to my own room.

I did not rest easy until about an hour later when I heard Mr. Remington and Mr. Cole talking in the hallway and calling out "good night" to one another. Even then, I kept recalling the sudden appearance in the nursery doorway of the woman in white.

Each time, I shuddered at the memory.

❦

I slept fitfully for about an hour, my dreams haunted by suddenly appearing apparitions who would awake me with a start. Around midnight, a beeping sound roused me and I sat straight up in bed. I threw off my covers and ran through the nursery sitting room to Cadence's room, where she was sleeping soundly.

The beeping grew louder and more insistent. It sounded like a smoke detector. I needed to wake Mr. Remington.

I quickly went to open the door leading to his study but withdrew my hand from the doorknob with a cry. The door was burning hot!

I tried the hallway door. It was cool to the touch. I opened it and then, shutting it behind me, raced down the hall to Mr. Remington's bedroom.

I pounded on the door, shouting, "Mr. Remington! Mr. Remington!"

Not waiting for his reply, I shoved the door open. Smoke

poured into his bedroom from the open study door, where I could see flames devouring his desk.

"Mr. Remington!" I screamed. "Wake up! There's a fire!"

He lay on his bed, senseless—perhaps overcome by the fumes. I shook him furiously.

"Mr. Remington! Ethan! Get up!" I pleaded. "Ethan!"

His eyes popped open with a look of curious surprise. "Jillian?"

"Quick! Get up! There's a fire!"

He leapt up.

I ran out into the hallway and grabbed a fire extinguisher. I had passed by it many times before without consciously noticing, but its presence had now come to my mind with vivid clarity. Covering my mouth and nose with one hand, I rushed back into his room.

Mr. Remington had yanked down some drapes and was beating the flames on his study desk. I aimed the extinguisher and smothered the rest with thick foam.

Between us, we managed to quench the fire. Panting and coughing, we viewed the damage. His beautiful cherry desk and credenza were blackened; his computer, melted; and stacks of files and papers, reduced to ashes.

"The baby!" he suddenly cried. He pulled on the connecting doorknob and yelped with pain. Using a drape to protect his hand, he gingerly opened the door and then rushed to her crib.

"Thank God," he murmured, gathering her in his arms. He looked at me then.

"Jillian, are you all right?"

I realized I must have been quite a sight. My long hair hung loose down to my waist. I wore a T-shirt top and plaid flannel pajama bottoms. But then he also was dressed for bed, wearing only pajama pants.

"Are you all right?" he repeated.

I caught myself staring at him. "Yes!" I replied, glancing down at my bare feet. "But you." I tried to turn the attention from myself. "Your hand. Did you burn it on the door?"

"The door—thank God I put in those fire doors. The baby, when I think what could have happened to her . . ." He hugged her more tightly.

"Did you burn your hand?"

"It's nothing. I'll put some ice on it and it will be fine. First, let's move Cadence to your room. All right? Is there any smoke in there?"

"No, I don't think so."

"Good. Here, take her," he said, handing her over almost reluctantly. "I'll move her crib."

"I'll wake up the Browns to help you."

"No, don't. I don't want to alarm anyone. I can manage." He began to pull on the crib and then winced.

"Wait," I said. "I'll help you. Let me put Cadence in my bed first." I quickly carried her into my room and laid her on her back in the center of my bed, barricading her in with pillows. Mr. Remington was tugging the crib with one hand. I slipped over to the opposite side and pushed it into my room.

"There." I gently transferred Cadence back to the crib, taking care not to wake her. "Now, let me see your hand." I took his hand in mine and examined his palm. "You have some blisters forming. Run some cold water on it before it gets worse."

I turned on the faucet over my washbasin and let the water run. "I'll go get some ice. There's a mini-fridge in the bar in the dining room, isn't there? Maybe there's some ice there."

"No," he commanded as he thrust his injured hand into the cold water. "I'll get it. There's something I need to check on, anyway." He dabbed the burn gingerly with a towel. "Jillian, I need you to stay here alone with the baby for a little while. Lock all the doors. The connecting door to the nursery too. If you hear or see anything amiss, call down to the gatehouse. Understand?"

I nodded and locked the doors behind him. I sat and waited for what seemed hours, but by the clock was little more than thirty minutes. During that time, I recalled all the details of the fire. I began to shake from the trauma and the cold.

Finally, I heard him softly call my name, and I jumped up to unlock the door and let him in.

"Everything all right?" he asked.

I nodded weakly, clasping my arms to my chest to control my shaking.

"Sit down," he ordered. "My word, what's wrong? You're cold? Or is it shock? Here." He took off the leather jacket he had donned over his pajamas and placed it around my shoulders. He knelt beside me and looked me in the eyes. "Are you all right, Jillian? You aren't hurt?"

"No, I'm fine."

"I'm sorry to have left you so long. Tell me, do you have any idea how the fire started? Did you see anyone or hear anything?"

"Just the smoke detector beeping. I was having trouble sleeping anyway. Was there fire anywhere else? Is everyone else all right? What about Mr. Cole?"

"Calvin is fine. He's on the other corridor so he didn't hear anything. I talked to Doug Crooke, the night porter, and he's doing a sweep of the castle now. But no, there's no more fire. It seems it was limited to my study."

"Who would do such a thing, and how did they get in?"

"We think perhaps one of the visitors for the candlelight tour must have wandered upstairs with a candle and dropped it."

This did not seem like a satisfactory answer to me. But then I remembered the mysterious woman in white.

"I did see someone upstairs during the tour, and she did seem lost. But she did not have a candle, and I told her that she was in the private quarters and watched her go back downstairs. So it couldn't have been her. I can't understand why anyone would wander up to your study. How could they have gotten in? It's as if they were looking for you. Oh, Ethan," I cried, "you could have been killed!"

"Yes, but for you." Suddenly, he smiled. "You know, you just called me 'Ethan.'"

"I'm sorry—Mr. Remington."

"No, I want you to, remember? It's only fitting that you call me by my Christian name now that you have saved my life. And you did save my life, you know. Our lives," he corrected, glancing at his daughter. "I will be forever indebted to you." He took my hands in his. "Thank you, Jillian. I don't like to be beholden to anyone. But, for some reason I don't mind being so to you." He would not release my hands but rubbed them gently. "I told you that you were good for me. Now you have saved me twice."

"I would do anything to help you," I said with the utmost sincerity.

"Anything?" He smiled sadly. "No, I don't think so. You would not go against your conscience."

I could not deny that and said nothing.

Still he held my hands.

"How is your burn?" I asked.

"Ah, not too bad." He did let go then as he examined his injured hand. "I'll put some more ice on it before bed."

"Where will you sleep?"

"I'll use one of the spare bedrooms upstairs."

"Mrs. Poole!" I exclaimed, suddenly remembering her.

"She's fine. Not to worry. Your quick thinking with the fire extinguisher saved us all."

He had been kneeling before me all this while. Now he slowly stood. "I suppose I should let you try to get some sleep before everyone wakes and the house is in an uproar."

I also stood. "Your jacket."

"Keep it. Are you all right now? No more trembling?" He lifted my chin and searched my face. "You know, I think I'll sleep next door on a couch in the family drawing room. Then I'll be just on the other side of the wall from you. If you hear anything, anything at all, or if you need me, just knock on the wall. All right?"

"All right," I said.

"Good night, my dear—good night, Jillian."

He seemed reluctant to leave, and I was reluctant to let him go.

"Good night . . . Ethan."

"Good night, Jillian," he repeated. "And a million thanks."

He took my hands in his again and suddenly pressed his lips to my palm. And then he was gone.

11

The next morning I hardly knew whether I wanted to see Mr. Remington or not. My ambivalence grew out of a desire to renew the intensity of feeling I had sensed between us the previous night, and the fear that I had merely fabricated it. Surely, a man of Mr. Remington's means would not foster fond affection for his daughter's nanny, and yet . . .

And yet, he had taken my hands in his, he had caressed them, he had pressed them to his lips. I relived that moment over and over in my mind. He had called me "my dear" and had been reluctant to leave me. Surely all that spoke of a genuine fondness.

My own infatuation had grown to a deeper admiration and affection. I could no longer deny to myself that I was in love with Ethan Remington. There were many reasons why I shouldn't allow myself to be, but nevertheless, I was.

As I dressed Cadence, I thought of all the questions I would like to ask him at breakfast. Questions about the search for CC, whether or not he thought there was a connection between CC and the fire, if the security guards had found any clues as to the cause of the fire. My litany of questions grew with my impatience to be with him.

But I was to be disappointed. Mr. Remington did not appear at breakfast. Evidently, he had left for London with Mr. Cole quite early in the morning.

I learned this from the servants, whom I found busily cleaning out his room and study. I heard their voices and the sounds of furniture being moved as I walked down the hallway with Cadence. We stopped and looked in the open door at a flurry of activity.

I spied Karla washing the smoke-blackened windowpanes.

"Hi, Karla. What's happened here?" I asked.

She glanced at me and resumed rubbing the glass. "Hello, Jillian. Didn't you hear anything last night?"

I ignored her question and repeated mine. "What happened?"

"Seems that one of the guests must have been overly nosey and carried a candle up into the master's study. Maybe they heard someone coming and dropped it in fright. Anyway, we found a silver candlestick in the middle of his desk. What a mess, eh? It's a good thing Mr. Remington installed those fire doors so it didn't spread, and that he put extinguishers about the house. He was able to put the fire out."

"By himself?"

"Yes. That's what I heard, anyway. I'm glad you weren't disturbed and that the baby is all right."

"Yes, me too. Karla, why do they think one of the guests caused the fire?"

"They don't think anyone else would be so careless. Besides"—she leaned over to me and whispered—"I saw the security guard, Mr. Crooke, come out of the spiral stairwell carrying a white shawl. I think that our culprit must have dropped it there. I'm sure Mr. Crooke is studying those surveillance tapes now to see if he can identify them."

"I saw a tall woman in a white shawl last night!" I exclaimed.

Karla looked at me eagerly. "Did you get a good look at her face?"

"No. She had it covered with the shawl."

"I would tell Mr. Crooke about it."

I watched her cleaning for a few minutes while I thought. "Karla," I said, "on which spiral staircase did Mr. Crooke find the shawl? The Laughing Cavalier's?"

"No, that's the funny thing. It was the hidden one from the boardroom up to Mr. Remington's study."

"How would someone know it was there?"

"That's what I was wondering. They said it was probably

just a curious guest trying doors and sneaking around. Some people are like that—always going where it's roped off. But to be honest"—her voice dropped to a whisper again—"I wonder if it weren't a staff member. Somebody who knows their way around. That's why I asked if you had seen her face."

"No, but why would a staff member do such a thing? No one is disgruntled with Mr. Remington, I hope. He's so considerate of his workers and pays them well. I just don't understand it."

"I don't think anyone wanted to hurt Mr. Remington. I think maybe they were trying to steal something. Some people have secret drug habits, you know, and they'll do anything for a fix. Even bite the hand that feeds them."

"But why go to his study? Surely there are more valuable objects to steal elsewhere in the castle."

"And easily traceable. Maybe they wanted access to his computer files or thought that he keeps some cash up there. I don't know. I'm just trying to figure it out."

"Women don't tend to do that kind of thing," I said.

Karla shrugged. "Maybe it wasn't a woman. You said she was tall, but you didn't see her face. The shawl thing could have been some sort of disguise. Did you see any hands or feet?"

I shook my head. "No. I didn't notice the shoes, and she was wearing gloves."

"See? That would go with my thief theory. No finger-prints."

I laughed then. "Honestly, Karla, maybe you should be a detective."

She smiled. "It would beat washing windows. I love a good mystery, and detective shows on the telly are my favorites."

I left her then as Cadence had become restless and was demanding her breakfast. As we walked through the suite of rooms, I scrutinized each worker to see if I could recognize the form of the woman in white. Most were too short or stout.

The exception was Mrs. Poole. She stood tall and slender, stretching her long arms up to rehang some draperies. I started at the sight and then gathered my courage.

"Mrs. Poole," I greeted her. "You're doing double duty today."

"Aye. But I don't mind. I don't want Mr. Ethan to have to sleep in the drawing room again."

"Did you hear or see anything last night?"

"Nay. All was quiet upstairs. I didn't wake up until Mr. Ethan pounded on my door in the wee hours to check on me."

"And were you all right?"

"I was quite fine. Just felt badly for Mr. Ethan. And what of you? Are you all right?"

"I'm fine. Just a little shaken."

She smiled at me, dispelling my suspicions. "You were a right brave lass from what Mr. Ethan told me," she said in a low voice. "Everyone else thinks he put out the fire, but I know it was your quick thinking that saved the day. We're indebted to you."

"It was nothing," I said, ashamed of my distrust. "You would have done the same."

"Aye, I would have to save Mr. Ethan and Miss Cadence. But you did it all the same. Thank ye for it."

I nodded in acknowledgment and left the room with more questions than answers. *So, was the woman in white the culprit? Was she related to CC? And who could she be?*

And then again, could she really be a he?

⁂

I had hoped to put my questions to Mr. Remington myself, but to my great disappointment, I did not encounter him anywhere. Nor, as was his habit, did he drop by the nursery to check on Cadence any time during the entire day.

When I left her in Mrs. Poole's charge for my afternoon run, I stopped by the gatehouse to speak to Mr. Crooke. The irony of his name had not escaped me, but his capable and trustworthy demeanor belied that association.

He greeted me courteously. "Hello, Miss Jillian. How are you today? Survive your ordeal last night?"

"Yes, I'm fine, thank you. Have you discovered the identity of the arsonist yet?"

He frowned and answered cautiously. "We may have done.

Do you have any information to add? Mr. Remington said that you hadn't heard or seen anything prior to the fire alarm going off. Is that correct?"

"Yes. But I did see someone peculiar earlier during the candlelight tour. She—or possibly he—was dressed all in white and wore a white shawl around their head, almost like a veil. One of the maids said that you found such a shawl on the hidden staircase going from the boardroom up to Mr. Remington's study."

"That's right. You say you saw this person on the tour?"

"Yes. And I noticed her because she evidently did not wish for her face to be seen. At first, I wondered if she was a Muslim and the shawl was a burqua. But the dress was not typical of that religion. Then I thought perhaps she was dressed in costume for the tour, but the gown appeared more Victorian than Renaissance. In fact, it reminded me of the posters advertising Andrew Lloyd Webber's musical *The Woman in White*."

Mr. Crooke sucked in his breath sharply. "You don't say? Now, then, did you notice anything about her? Get a look at her face? Or anything?"

"No, the person was completely covered up—and even wore gloves. I couldn't say absolutely for sure if it was a woman or a man or even if their skin was fair or dark."

"Why would you think it could be a man?"

"I just couldn't say for sure it wasn't. I mean, the dress could have been a disguise just like the shawl. What I do know is that the person was tall—for a woman anyway—and slender."

"Did you have any conversation or encounter with the person?"

"Not exactly. I was always very aware of her. I thought she was staring at me—no, really staring at Cadence, and that she was following us around. I felt like she—or he—was stalking us. In fact, later when I took Cadence to the nursery, this person followed us."

Mr. Crooke sat up very straight and peered at me with an alert, penetrating gaze. "Followed you?"

"Yes, well, I'm not sure. What happened was this: I was rocking Cadence and giving her a bottle when I looked up and there she was—standing in the doorway like a ghost— just staring at us." I shuddered at the recollection.

"Blimey!" he exclaimed. "What then?"

"I said something like she shouldn't be there, that this was the private part of the house, and that she should go back downstairs."

"Did she say anything?"

"No. She went back down the main staircase. I followed her to be sure."

"Right. Well done."

"So, you think she's the arsonist, don't you? Did you see her on the surveillance tapes?"

"Yes, but of course, as you said, she—or he—was well disguised. Anyway, I appreciate hearing this and will pass it along to Mr. Remington. You've been very helpful, Miss Jillian."

"Will there still be a tour tonight?" I asked, unable to conceal my anxiety.

"Yes, but you needn't fear. We've hired an extra lot of security men who will be scattered throughout the castle and grounds. I will post someone at each staircase—including the hidden ones. As for you and Miss Cadence, I'd like you to stay put in the nursery tonight during the tour. And Mr. Remington requested that the little one sleep in your room for the rest of your stay here. I'll post a man in the hallway right outside your door. How does that suit you?"

"Thank you." I sighed with relief. "That sounds just fine to me."

Mr. Crooke was true to his word. I kept Cadence safely hidden away in the nursery for the evening, and according to Mr. Remington's instructions, put her down to sleep in the crib, which remained in my room. Even after all the guests had left and the security guards made a final sweep of the entire castle, one guard stayed outside our locked doors through the night. Neither were there further disturbances from the telephones. Mr. Remington had tapped his private phone and routed all calls through the gatehouse. The second candlelight tour transpired without incident, and afterward the castle closed its doors to tourists for the winter.

But it hardly stayed quiet. Over the weekend, it fairly simmered with the effervescence of the staff vigorously cleaning, scrubbing, airing out, rearranging, and decorating. I had thought the castle quite clean and beautifully decorated already, but Mr. Remington spared no expense or trouble in preparation for the movie premier fête. From the nursery windows, I watched as flambeau torches were placed around the circular drive on the front lawn and strands of lights were draped like garlands from the casements. Florists, caterers, decorators, and various workers came and went.

The only person who did not come and go was he I longed to see most. That longing was not to be satisfied until the actual premier party. Even then, when I finally laid eyes on him again, he was arm in arm with the stunning Brittany Graham.

12

The hubbub of preparation for the premier party continued even as we heard the arriving vehicles rumbling over the moat bridge and crunching over the gravel circular drive. The World War II–era limousines and army jeeps used in Mr. Remington's film doubled now as a taxi service, shuttling their dazzling occupants from the car park to the front hallway of the castle. The lights strung from the casements twinkled merrily while the tunes of Tommy Dorsey, played by a big band orchestra, beckoned the guests to swing dance in the banqueting hall.

The nursery windows, set right over the entry doors, afforded the perfect vantage to watch the arrivals. Holding Cadence, Mrs. Poole stood beside me as we gazed at the galaxy of stars emerging from their cars into the warm glow of the flambeaux.

"What lovely gowns!" exclaimed Mrs. Poole. "Everyone

looks so handsome, don't they? I wish we could have gone to the cinema to see the film. Then we would know who's who."

"Yes. It would have been fun to see it."

"Oh well. We're paid by Mr. Remington to mind the home front, not go to the cinema. Now, you and Cadence should be going downstairs, don't you think?"

I sighed. "I'd rather not go down. I wish I could just watch things from up here. I'll feel so conspicuous with all those beautiful people."

"They'll be looking at Cadence and won't even notice you."

"Would you like to take her down, Mrs. Poole? You could see all those pretty gowns close up."

"Me? No. Besides, Mr. Ethan left explicit instructions for you to bring Cadence to the grand drawing room. You should get going."

"How do I look?" I wore the black cocktail dress that Corinne had helped me select and had French braided my hair.

"Fine. The basic black will serve you well in remaining inconspicuous. If you want to avoid having to make a grand entrance, take Cadence down via the private staircase. Then you can duck in the back of the drawing room before anyone notices you."

"Good idea," I said, taking Cadence from her. "Isn't she cute?"

Her newly washed dark curls shone, as did her bright blue

eyes. She looked adorable in her green velvet dress, white tights, and patent leather shoes.

"Aye. I told you everyone will be watching her and won't even notice you."

"Well, wish me luck."

"You'll be fine," she assured me. "Now go. Mr. Ethan likes everyone to be punctual."

I carried Cadence past the Laughing Cavalier and down the spiral staircase. The sounds of laughter, animated conversation, and the clinking of glasses mingled with the big band strains coming from speakers placed about the castle. I slipped in the back of the drawing room as suggested and retired to a window seat where I would not be on display but could still survey the entire room.

Cadence, entranced by the kaleidoscope of colors and sounds, babbled excitedly as she pointed her chubby fingers here and there. I hoped she would stay contentedly on my lap and not put up a fuss for me to put her down. I did not relish the thought of having to chase her about the crowded room. For the time being, she did acquiesce to sit still.

That gave me ample opportunity to indulge in observing the assembly. But there was only one person I really wanted to see. I quickly found him.

And her.

The beautiful Miss Brittany Graham. In her strappy high heels, she stood nearly as tall as Mr. Remington. Her shoulder-length black hair did not cover the plunging décolletage of her deep purple gown. A platinum and amethyst necklace nestled alluringly in her cleavage. Everything about her demanded to be noticed, admired, and desired. She clung to Mr. Remington, whispered in his ear, and laughed with him as though sharing secret jokes. Society column photographers furiously snapped pictures.

From my vantage, I could observe them for some time. I was puzzled by what I saw. They seemed enthralled with one another, and yet her affect lacked sincerity, her laughter sounded forced. Could a man of Mr. Remington's intelligence and insight fall prey to someone who was merely playing a part?

Cadence began to squirm. I wondered if it might be possible to set her down near her father and then slink quietly away. It wasn't.

"Where's Cadence?" I heard his rich baritone voice rise above the crowd. "I want you to meet her."

"I think she's sitting over in the window seat with her nanny," said Miss Graham. "Honestly, Ethan. Why don't you remarry? Then perhaps you could get rid of the nanny. It's so hard to get decent ones these days—especially ones who won't sleep with their employers."

Mr. Remington laughed. "Is that such a bad thing?"

"Ethan! You rogue." She feigned shock and then laughed too. "Really, though. It's time you remarried."

"And whom should I marry, my pretty one?"

She smiled and lowered her eyes like a practiced coquette. "I can think of someone."

"I'm sure you can."

He looked toward me and called, "Miss Dare, please bring Cadence here to me."

I rose and gently put Cadence down, steadying her before whispering, "Go see Daddy."

"Da-da!" she cried as she toddled across the room to him.

With a collective murmur and declarations of, "Isn't she precious? What a darling child!" the assemblage parted to give her passage.

Mr. Remington caught her up in his open arms and tickled her with a profusion of kisses. "Hello, baby girl, I've missed you. Did you miss Daddy?"

She answered him with her own sloppy kiss.

"Brittany, this is my daughter, Cadence."

"You don't say?" she replied with a hint of sarcasm.

Fascinated by the dangling jewels, Cadence made a grab for Miss Graham's necklace. Mr. Remington swung her away. "No, no, darling."

"Maybe you should call her nanny over here," Miss Graham said as she clutched her necklace.

The photographers moved in closer to capture this new subject. The young actress, leaning her head against Mr. Remington's shoulder, smiled and feigned an interest in the baby.

I watched and waited. Feeling a tap on my shoulder, I glanced up to see Mr. Cole standing by my side.

"Jillian," he said. "I think you should take Cadence. Ethan's not thinking straight, allowing her to be photographed by the paparazzi."

"But he may not want me to."

"Come with me."

I followed him over to Mr. Remington's circle.

"Ah, Jillian!" Mr. Remington declared when he saw me approach. "I'd like to introduce you to Miss Brittany Graham, the fabulous star of *Evasions*. Brittany, this is Cadence's nanny, Jillian Dare."

She was even more glamorous close up.

"Nice to meet you," I said, extending my hand.

She nodded, but rather than taking my proffered hand, she addressed Mr. Cole. "Calvin, how are you, darling? Did you enjoy the film?"

"Very much," he replied. "Outstanding job. Kudos to all."

"Thanks, Cal," said Mr. Remington. "Now, Jillian, I would like you to meet Brittany's costar, the dashing Brendan Michaels. Brendan, this is Cadence's nanny, Jillian Dare." He introduced a very handsome young man with thick fair hair and captivatingly blue eyes. I must confess, I hadn't noticed him before, so focused had I been on Mr. Remington and Miss Graham.

Brendan Michaels smiled and offered his hand. "Hello, there."

I took it. "Hi. Nice to meet you."

"And you. And this is my wife, Amy." He proudly draped his left arm around a petite woman whose well-coiffed shoulder-length auburn hair framed a delicate and pretty face.

"Hello," she said with a hint of shyness. "Ethan's baby is so sweet. Is she a good baby?"

"Yes, she is."

"My wife is fascinated with babies." Brendan leaned toward me confidingly. "We're expecting."

"Congratulations!" I said warmly.

"Thank you," they both rejoined, beaming happily.

I now understood why Brittany was not showering her attentions on her obviously claimed costar. Nevertheless, she was not hesitating to practice all her feminine allurements on her wealthy producer.

Calvin Cole was whispering something in Mr. Remington's ear. I could tell by the frown on his face that Mr. Remington did not like what he was hearing.

He held up his hand and commanded in a loud, authoritative voice, "No more pictures of the baby. And you do not have permission to publish any photos of her. Of course, you may take all you wish of our stars Brittany Graham and Brendan Michaels."

He then called to me over the buzz of renewed conversation.

"Jillian, please take Cadence. It's her bedtime."

I quickly complied. Miss Graham seemed relieved to have the baby literally out of the picture as the photographers continued to snap away. I observed the actress bending her head toward Mr. Remington's, speaking and laughing softly in an intimate way, and linking her arm in his.

I felt sick at heart.

What a fool I had been! I berated myself and my false hopes as I carried the baby back through the crush of beautiful people and up the back staircase to my room.

How can you for a moment have pretended to yourself that he is interested in you? You are just a poor, plain nanny. Nothing more. She is gorgeous and talented—even if she isn't very nice. She is all a man of means like Ethan Remington would need as a trophy wife.

But a trophy wife was all she would be. She certainly had not demonstrated any maternal sentiments or genuine interest in Cadence. And she hardly seemed to be a kindred spirit to Mr. Remington. I honestly did not believe she could make him happy—at least for long.

The party, with its sounds of merriment, drifted late into the night. About one o'clock, I heard Mr. Remington, Mr. Cole, and Miss Graham talking and laughing in the hallway and then their muted voices in the family drawing room next to my bedroom. I found it difficult to sleep. Finally, around two, all fell silent.

I couldn't help but wonder if Mr. Remington was sleeping alone or with Miss Graham. Of course, it was none of my business, but the thought plagued me nonetheless.

❧

I had the next day off and had arranged to go sightseeing with Karla in London. I was glad to be absent from Keswick Hall while Mr. Remington was entertaining his guests. He had planned for them to golf, ride horseback, and boat on the lake, and the fine weather cooperated.

The sun also shone on our sightseeing excursion. Like many native city dwellers, Karla had never before bothered to visit London's landmarks and tourist destinations, and so she was quite game for taking the London guided bus tour with me and seeing the Tower of London, the Houses of Parliament, Westminster Abbey, and the Globe Theatre. We both enjoyed the river cruise with its wryly humorous commentary as we sailed from the Tower to Westminster. We took the Tube over to Covent Garden, where we ate our supper while watching the street performers. Later we threaded our way through crowded lanes to a cinema in Leicester Square, where we saw Mr. Remington's new film, *Evasions*. We were both enthralled.

"I'm in love with Brendan Michaels," Karla announced as we made our way back to the subway. "Do you think I could get his autograph? His eyes are so gorgeous!"

"They are," I agreed. "But he's happily married, you know, and they're expecting a baby."

"I can still be in love with him. It will just have to be unrequited. Did you get to meet him?"

"Yes, and his wife too. They were very nice."

"And what of the beautiful Brittany Graham? Was she nice?"

"I'm sure she is."

"You don't sound very convincing."

"I don't? Well, I was just introduced to her. I wasn't actually able to talk to her."

"Do you think she and Mr. Remington are an item?"

"I believe she thinks so."

"Apparently, the tabloids do too. Look at these headlines." Karla pulled a daily paper out of its rack at a newsstand. "'*Evasions* star and producer: blooming off-screen romance.' And this: 'Remington steals starlet's heart!' And this one: 'Brittany & Ethan: our hottest new couple!'" She picked the *Daily Times Mirror* and paid the street vendor.

As we descended the escalator into the Tube station, we passed scores of posters plastered on the walls advertising various shows and films. Karla spotted numerous ones for *Evasions*, which elicited her cries of, "Brendan Michaels is so gorgeous! Maybe you could ask Mr. Remington if he could give me a poster. It's so exciting that he has become a movie producer—much more so than being a telecommunications exec. All those celebrities! I'm glad they're staying on for another day. Maybe I will get that autograph."

I smiled at her enthusiasm, but then my breath caught in my throat. We walked by some posters advertising the musical *The Woman in White*. I felt chilled remembering the strange apparition who appeared so suddenly at the nursery door the night of the fire.

"Karla," I said, "did you see the pictures of *The Woman in White*? That's what the figure I saw the night of the fire looked like. She was wearing a dress like that."

Karla stared at the posters and then at me. "You're joking, right?" she asked in a slow, serious voice.

"No, why would I joke about that? She was rather frightening."

"Right. She was dressed in a long gown like that?"

"Yes, it was definitely Victorian in style and all in white and reminded me of the pictures I had seen of the musical. It seemed odd at the time, but then I thought that perhaps she meant to fit in with the costumes of the performers for the candlelight tour."

"That makes sense. People like to dress up for such events. Did you mention what she looked like to Mr. Crooke like I suggested?"

"Yes."

"Did you tell him the bit about *The Woman in White*?"

"Yes."

"Good. I'm sure every clue helps. I wonder if they'll be able to find the culprit."

"I hope so," I said with warmth. "I would feel a whole lot safer."

"Yes, but now that Mr. Remington has beefed up the security detail, I don't think you need to worry. It won't happen again."

On our train ride back to Maidstone, Karla devoured the tabloid gossip, sharing tidbits with me now and then. I tried to assume indifference but was burning with curiosity.

"Honestly," she said, "do you think this stuff about Mr. Remington and Brittany Graham is for real?"

"I wouldn't know," I answered.

"But his wife—"

"Mr. Remington is bound to remarry someday," I said philosophically.

"But to Brittany Graham?"

I was gratified that Karla seemed nearly as opposed to the idea as I was.

"These showbiz marriages don't tend to last long," she said. "You would think he'd go for someone more stable, who would be a good mother for Cadence."

You would think so, wouldn't you? I silently agreed. *But would Mr. Remington?*

13

⌒⌒⌒

I paid the taxi driver and gathered up the parcels I had acquired in London. My excursion with Karla had granted me the opportunity for some Christmas shopping. At the Tower of London's gift shop, I had bought a soft, blue Shetland wool pullover for my friend Diane Brooke, a sage green one for Sharon, T-shirts for the other Brooke children, Royal Doulton china teacups and saucers for their mother and for Mrs. Carter, a Burberry scarf for Corinne, tins of tea for Jack and Marta, and a soft wooly stuffed lamb for Cadence. I had already devised a surprise gift for Mr. Remington.

When I stopped at the gatehouse at Keswick Hall to gain admittance through the postern door, Mr. Crooke came out to speak to me.

"'Evening, Miss Jillian. Did you have a nice visit to London?"

"Yes, sir, I did."

"Very good. Well, now, Mr. Remington has requested that you go to him immediately on your return. I believe you will find the party in the billiard room."

"Okay, thanks. I'll go there now." I hesitated and then asked, "Mr. Crooke, has there been any progress on finding the arsonist?"

"Yes, although I'm not really at liberty to talk about the investigation."

"I understand. Good night, Mr. Crooke."

"Good night, Miss Jillian. And sleep tight. No worries. We're keeping a good watch out for you."

I hurried through the postern and across the front lawn to the private entrance to Keswick Hall. Letting myself in with my security card, I put the packages down in the foyer and hung up the leather jacket Mr. Remington had so thoughtfully bought for me. I wished I could have taken the time to tidy my appearance—I had been gone since early that morning—but took comfort in the fact that at least I had dressed decently in black dress slacks and a red sweater, even if I had my hair pulled back in a simple ponytail. Mr. Remington had requested that I go to him right away, and I never liked to keep him waiting.

Not wanting to interrupt the guests until my presence had been acknowledged, I stood in the doorway of the billiard room. Brendan and Amy Michaels, Brittany Graham,

Calvin Cole, and others whom I had not met stood about the billiard table or lounged in chairs nearby. The atmosphere seemed relaxed and congenial.

I watched as Miss Graham touched Mr. Remington's arm. "Ethan," she said, "that dreadful little nanny of yours is standing there. What could she possibly want with you at this hour?"

He looked up sharply and strode over to me. "Come in, Jillian. Why didn't you let me know that you were here?"

"I didn't want to interrupt you."

"Come in."

"I'd rather not."

His eyes held mine. "So you overheard Brittany's careless remark?"

"Yes, sir."

"Don't pay her any mind. She doesn't mean anything by it."

"Still, I'm tired and would like to go to bed. Mr. Crooke said you wanted to see me about something?"

"Did you have a good day in London?" he asked.

"Yes, sir."

"What did you see?"

"The Tower, the new Globe, and Westminster. We also took the bus tour and the river cruise, had dinner in Covent Garden, and went to see *Evasions* in Leicester Square."

"Busy day! How did you like the film?"

"Both Karla and I enjoyed it very much. She wondered if she could possibly have one of the publicity posters. She

137

would also be thrilled if she could have Mr. Michaels's autograph."

He smiled, pleased with this reaction. "Of course. This Karla—isn't she one of the chambermaids?"

"Yes, sir. An upstairs maid."

"Right. I'll take care of it."

"Thank you. Now, you wanted to see me about something?"

"Ah yes. Let's step into the hallway." He took my elbow and led me out of earshot of his guests. "I'm sorry to spring this on you, but I've made a change in plans. I'd like for you and Cadence to fly back to the States with Calvin tomorrow morning."

"Tomorrow?" I was admittedly disappointed to have my UK visit thus cut short.

"Right. I apologize for the late notice. I have to stay a few more days to wrap up some things, but I thought it would be a good idea, now that the premier festivities are over, for Cadence to be safely back at home. Since Calvin is flying back tomorrow, I would like you two to go with him. I am frankly uneasy about her being here after the recent unpleasantness."

I wondered if he also wished to spend more time alone with Brittany Graham.

"I've already changed the tickets and notified Aunt Elise. I'll drive you myself to the airport early tomorrow morning," he was saying. "I'm afraid we'll have to leave at five. I know that doesn't give you much time, so again I apologize. I've asked Mrs. Poole to pack Cadence's things so that you'll only have to be concerned about yourself."

Once again, he had demonstrated undue thoughtfulness on a mere servant's behalf.

"Thank you. I'll be ready."

"Excellent!" he said. "I'll send a valet up to retrieve your bags at 4:45."

"All right. I'd better begin packing. Good night."

He took my hands in his.

"Jillian," he said. "Again, I'm sorry for the late notice, and hope this hasn't disappointed or inconvenienced you too much."

He hesitated and then added, "I'm also sorry that Cadence—and you—have to leave me. But trust me, it's really for the best."

I swallowed my disappointment and mustered a smile.

"Ethan!" Brittany Graham trilled from the billiard room. "You're neglecting us!"

"I'll be right there!" he called back. With a quick squeeze of my hand, he said, "Good night, Jillian. Try to get some sleep. Have Cadence ready to go at five."

"Good night," I said with a sigh, and hastened off to pack.

❧

I stayed up until nearly midnight in order to pack my clothes and fit in the gifts I had bought, and then set the alarm for four so that I could have Cadence and myself ready when the valet came to pick up our suitcases. While we were gathering in the foyer to put on our coats, the valet had brought Mr. Remington's silver Aston Martin from the car park to the side entrance, loaded the luggage, and secured the baby's car seat.

As Mr. Remington drove us around the circular drive and over the moat bridge, I looked back with ambivalence to Keswick Hall standing regally in a shroud of mist and mystery. The predawn darkness not being conducive to sightseeing, I closed my eyes to catch a nap while Cadence soon fell asleep in the car seat beside me. In the front of the car, Mr. Remington and Mr. Cole conversed in hushed tones.

Suddenly, I was jolted awake by the screeching of brakes and squealing of tires. The car swung madly around and flung itself against a tree. Almost simultaneously, I heard the shatter of glass and the pop of deployed air bags, followed by a moment of eerie silence.

"What the devil!" shouted Mr. Remington. "Is everyone all right?"

Cadence bawled loudly in shocked outrage.

"I'm fine," I managed to choke out. "Could you turn on the lights so I can see Cadence?"

He did and emitted a groan. "Blast! Cal! Oh, God have mercy. Cal?"

I found that none of the impact had affected Cadence other than violently awakening her. "The baby's fine!" I called out as I soothed her cries with her pacifier.

"Thank God. Cal?"

I heard Mr. Remington unbuckle his seat belt and watched as he pushed back the air bags to tend to his friend. I was sickened to see the front passenger window shattered. Mr. Cole's door had smashed into the tree. Mine had escaped unscathed although I felt bruised and sore. Evidently, Mr. Cole's head had hit the window seconds before the air bags deployed. He was bleeding profusely.

"Cal? Talk to me, mate." Mr. Remington took a handkerchief from his pocket and dabbed at the blood. Mr. Cole moaned.

"Thank God, you're alive. I think I found the main cut. Jillian, get out on Cadence's side and come up here. I want you to hold this on his forehead. We must staunch the bleeding. You're not squeamish, are you?"

I was, but I knew I had to think of Mr. Cole's comfort above my own. "I can do it," I said as I unbuckled my seat belt and scooted past the car seat. I opened the driver's side door and, squeezing in front of Mr. Remington, placed my hand over his where he pressed the handkerchief against Mr. Cole's wound.

"Good girl," he said as he gently slid his hand away and then switched off the engine. "I'll ring 999 for help."

As he stepped out of the car, I could hear the bleep, bleep, bleep of his phone as he pounded out the number.

"This is Ethan Remington. I need an ambulance right away on the north drive from Keswick Hall. There's been an auto accident and a man is hurt. Tell the rescue squad that they are not to use any sirens on the estate property. Do you understand? No sirens! Good. That's right, the north drive. We're about a furlong from the Fairfax gate. Now hurry!"

Then I heard him dial another number. "Brown? Ethan Remington. I want you to bring the Bentley up to the Fairfax gate. I'll need you to drive Miss Dare and Cadence to the airport. My car has met with an accident, and I don't want them to miss their plane. Do not speak to anyone of this. Just come right away."

He poked his head into the car. "How are you doing, Jillian? Can you stop the bleeding?"

"Yes, I think the pressure is helping. Should we have him lie down?"

"No, the rescue squad will determine what's best to be done. They should be here shortly."

He slumped down on the edge of the seat. "I'm so sorry, Cal. I don't know what could have happened. I wasn't speeding and I didn't swerve to avoid hitting anything. All of a sudden we just flew off the road."

"Check the tires." Mr. Cole's quiet command startled me.

Mr. Remington reacted similarly. "What did you say?"

"Check the tires," he repeated.

"Right. There should be a torch in the boot." Mr. Remington climbed back out of the car, opened the car trunk, removed a flashlight, and examined the tires.

"Blast!" I heard him exclaim. "Blast! Blast!" He came around and leaned back into the driver's side. "You won't believe this. There's a pocketknife stuck in the front tire on your side. The tire's completely blown."

"She's trying to kill you, Ethan," Mr. Cole said in the same quiet, labored voice. "Or someone. She could have killed Cadence and us too. She's got to be stopped."

"That's enough, Cal! We don't have any evidence it's her."

"Hire a PI and take out a restraining order. Next time she may succeed. We should sue her at the very least."

"Just stop! I'm doing all I can, you know that. Now, not another word. I mean it!"

My hand began to tremble, whether from the strain of pressing down on the wound or from the effects of the accident and the words I had overheard, I couldn't be sure. What I could be certain of was the fact that they knew or thought they knew who was behind all the sinister events. Moreover, for some reason, Mr. Remington did not want to enlighten me.

After the longest passage of ten minutes I had ever experienced, the ambulance arrived without the fanfare of sirens as Mr. Remington had stipulated. They quickly attended to Mr. Cole and examined Mr. Remington, Cadence, and me as well. A police squad car pulled up and walked around the car, taking notes and photographs. I overheard Mr. Remington forcefully requesting the police officers not to release any pictures or information to the press.

The ambulance prepared to transport Mr. Cole to a nearby hospital. Thankfully, his injuries were superficial, not life-threatening. In the meantime, Mr. Brown, the butler, had driven up in the Bentley and was calmly transferring the luggage and car seat. Mr. Remington buckled in Cadence with a profusion of kisses, and then encircled me with his arm while he walked me to the car door.

"My dear Jillian," he said kindly, "I'm so sorry. Thank God we've been spared a terrible tragedy. It's now more important than ever that you and Cadence go home to Virginia. Do you think you'll be all right?"

I felt badly shaken. I have admitted to a fear of automobile accidents, no doubt stemming from the death of my almost adoptive parents. But we had been spared, and I was thankful.

"Yes," I said. "But I can't help wishing you were going home with us."

He turned my face to him. "I wish I were too. Truly. And I'm sorry to send you on alone with Cadence. But I have business I must attend to, and now I must look after Calvin as well."

As he helped me into the car, he said, "Give my love to Aunt Elise. Tell her I'll be on the first plane home that I can. You won't even have time to recover from your jet lag before I'm back harassing you in the nursery."

He surprised me by gently kissing me on the forehead.

"Good-bye, my dear," he whispered. "I'll be home soon. I promise."

14

It was good to be home. For I now considered Carter Plantation as my home. As thrilling as it had been to travel abroad and to stay in an ancient English castle, I was happy to be back in Virginia among familiar surroundings and in the comfort and security of my own little suite of rooms. Mrs. Carter, Jack, and Marta greeted us with such warmth that I genuinely felt a part of the family. Even Corinne Cooke condescended to grant me a smile as she eagerly took Cadence from my arms.

Yes, it was good to be home. Good, and safe as well. I hadn't realized how much stress I had been under during my brief stay at Keswick Hall until I was far away from it. In Virginia, I did not worry about harassing phone calls, spooky appearances by a woman in white, life-threatening fires, or intentionally punctured tires. The eerie email messages had ceased weeks before when Mr. Remington had switched my account address. My only concern now was to have him safely back in Virginia with us. Whoever meant him harm was still on the loose in England and capable of inflicting more damage.

After Marta's delicious welcome-home dinner of fried chicken, mashed potatoes, green beans, and biscuits, followed by coffee and pecan pie, I retired—full and contented—to my rooms. I pulled out my journal, climbed into my four-poster bed, and settled against a pile of pillows.

Opening the journal to one of the back pages, I found the heading "Who Is CC?" Below that inscription, I crossed out the names of people I had previously suspected: Corinne Cooke and Calvin Cole. I then wrote the words, "Possible but not likely," and beneath that, the names Mr. Crooke and Mrs. Poole. In parentheses I put "Constance" next to Mrs. Poole for I had learned that to be her first name. After that, I drew a big question mark. Neither the security guard nor the nurse had acted at all guilty, but both had "C" names, both were tall and slender, and both had been on the premises during the time of the fire. I did not add Karla's name. Other than the fact that she had altered the spelling of her name, I had no reason to distrust her.

I was not any closer to discovering the identity of CC, although it had become evident that Mr. Remington and Mr. Cole both strongly suspected someone whom they referred to with a feminine pronoun. Why wouldn't they have shared their suspicion with the police? The mystery had only deepened. Yet, Mr. Remington had said he was doing all he could. I certainly hoped so. Concern for his safety and for Mr. Cole's recovery dominated my prayers that evening, and in truth, over the next few days, until they both returned safely home to Virginia.

Besides his absence, one other thing marred my homecoming: the gossip surrounding the alleged romance and anticipated marriage between Mr. Remington and Brittany Graham.

Corinne, especially, had been tantalized by photos she had seen in *People* magazine, and she couldn't wait to ask me for explicit descriptions of the premier party and the film's stars. She eagerly plied me with questions as to what everyone wore, how they styled their hair, who accompanied whom, how they acted, and so on. I tried to answer all her queries patiently, but my knowledge fell short of satisfying her desire for details.

"I'm sorry, Corinne, but I really didn't spend that much time with them."

"But do you think the tabloids are right?" she pressed. "Do you think Mr. Remington and Brittany Graham plan to get married?"

"Is that what the tabloids say here?" I asked with dismay.

"Yes. They say that they were constantly together in London and that the buzz is of a wedding in the works."

"Then maybe it's true. But I haven't heard anything about it."

"Were they constantly together?"

"Why, no. Not constantly. They were together often, but mostly for the film events."

"Didn't she stay at Keswick Hall?"

"Yes."

"With him?"

"Corinne!"

"I was just wondering . . ."

"It's really not our business, is it?"

"Oh, I don't know. Famous people are everyone's business. After all, it's our interest in their affairs that keeps them famous. Just tell me this: is Brittany as beautiful in person as she is in her photos?"

I thought of the gorgeous creature in the glamorous purple gown with the plunging décolletage and sighed. "Honestly, I think she's more beautiful in person."

Corinne sighed too with envy. "I wish I could have seen her. Was she nice?"

"She may be. I don't know. The truth is—she wasn't very nice to me."

"Hmm . . . that's not a good sign." Corinne thought for a while. "It makes me worry for Mr. Remington. I hope she's nice to him, and that she's not just after his money."

"Me too," I was quick to agree. "He deserves someone who will make him happy—especially after losing his wife."

Corinne's eyes narrowed. "Jillian, just what do you know about his wife?"

"Nothing really." I shrugged. "He hasn't wanted to talk about her."

"Yeah, that's right," she said slowly. "He doesn't want any of us to talk about her. So, let's change the subject. What did you see in London?"

The subject abruptly changed. We did not speak again of Mrs. Remington.

Mr. Remington was true to his word, returning to Carter Plantation just a few days after Cadence and I did. Needless to say, I was delighted to see him, and he seemed delighted to see me—or rather us.

Over the next few days, he frequently dropped by the nursery throughout the day. With the exception of a couple of evenings when he had to attend some Christmas parties on neighboring estates, he stayed home at night, helping me put Cadence to bed and then inviting me to join him and Mrs. Carter in the family room. I savored these times with him. Sitting near a cheery fire and sipping a glass of wine, he talked easily to me about his interest in history, travel, art, music, and film. He told me stories about his parents, his childhood, and his days at Oxford and Yale. Ethan Remington was a loquacious talker, and I was an enraptured listener.

He remained silent on only three subjects: his wife, Brittany Graham, and the mysterious CC.

On one of these pleasant evenings, he revealed a surprise for us.

"Guess where we're going tomorrow night?" he asked with a gleam in his eyes.

"Now, Ethan, please don't tell me you're leaving us again," Mrs. Carter fretted.

"No, dear aunt. Didn't you hear me say, 'Guess where *we're* going'? I'll tell you. I bought tickets for the three of us—you, Jillian, and myself—to go to Ford's Theatre in DC to see *A Christmas Carol.* How would you like that?"

"Ah! Tomorrow?" Mrs. Carter clapped her small hands together. "How marvelous! I haven't been downtown to a play in years."

"Good. I thought since Jillian is a fan of the classics, she'd enjoy seeing it too. Am I right, Jillian?"

"I'd love to go. It's very considerate of you, but who will take care of Cadence?"

"I've already asked Corinne Cooke to babysit. I'd like to leave here around four o'clock. We'll drive into town, see the National Christmas tree and some of the decorations around the Mall, get some dinner, and then catch the show. I thought it'd be a nice way to get into the Christmas spirit. So, will you ladies join me?"

We readily agreed to his plan. Promptly at four o'clock we climbed into the Cadillac Escalade for the ride into the city. Mr. Remington requested that I sit up front with him so that he could point out sights along the way. By the time we crossed the Potomac River from Arlington into the District, dusk had fallen and the city lights blazed from the national monuments over the wintry landscape. We drove by the Kennedy Center, the Lincoln Memorial, and the White House with its towering Christmas tree brilliantly lit and decorated in festive garb.

Mr. Remington treated us to a pre-performance dinner at an elegant but warm Tuscan restaurant close to Ford's Theatre. When we first settled into our orchestra seats in the small, intimate theatre, Mr. Remington pointed out to me the box seats, draped in black crepe and an American flag, where President Abraham Lincoln had watched a play the night he was shot by John Wilkes Booth. During the intermission, Mr. Remington led us downstairs to the special exhibit on the assassination, where Mrs. Carter and I were fascinated to view Lincoln's clothes and various historical artifacts.

At first I found it sad and discomforting to sit in the historic theatre where Lincoln had met his untimely end. Yet, we were soon transported by the spirited and talented cast of *A Christmas Carol* into Charles Dickens's wonderful and heartwarming tale of redemption, and we left the theatre with light hearts full of Christmas cheer.

We drove over the Roosevelt Bridge back into Virginia, leaving behind the bright lights of Washington, while Mr. Remington and I talked. Mrs. Carter quickly fell asleep in the backseat. As we conversed in the dark comfort of the car, I could almost pretend that we were on a date together.

"I'm glad we had a full meal before the show," Ethan said, "otherwise I would have wanted to jump up on the stage and devour that fabulous turkey dinner at the end. Didn't it look incredibly real? You could almost smell the stuffing."

"It did look good," I agreed. "You know, I read somewhere that when the play was staged in Dickens's time, they did use a real cooked dinner every night and fed the cast with it. Many of the cast members, especially the children, were orphans or street urchins, and the food was part of Dickens's way of paying them. One season, the stage manager was perplexed at how much of the dinner was going missing before the show was over each night. He finally figured out that the little girl who was playing Tiny Tim was taking her plate over to her stool by the fireside and passing the food through a hole into the waiting hands of her sister, who would take the food home to feed their family. He wanted to put a stop to it and spoke to Dickens about it, and Dickens's response was, 'Give the child the whole turkey!'"

"Really? That's a true story?"

"Yes, at least that's what I remember of it. I really like the fact that Dickens didn't just write about the poor. He actually did something about it."

"Right. Now let's say, for the sake of discussion, you were rich, Jillian. What would you do with your money? Would you use it to help the poor?"

"If I were rich? Let me see . . . If I were rich, I think I would probably give my money to my foster family the Brookes. They do so much to help others. And I would probably also want to support an orphanage or an organization that tries to help needy children."

Mr. Remington chuckled. "Would you give all your money away or would you keep just a little for yourself?"

I smiled. "I haven't grown up with much, so I don't really know what it would be like to have a lot of money. I think I can be happy with very little. But what about you? What charities do you support?"

He frowned. "I'm ashamed to say I haven't supported any to any great extent. Just the odd contribution here and there when called upon. I suppose I should give it some thought—especially after watching Ebenezer Scrooge's reformation tonight."

"Well, Christmas is the season for giving, so it may be the perfect time for you to think about it."

He grunted and then, after a few moments of silent reflection, said, "When we first met, Jillian, you termed your childhood as Dickensian. Would you care to elaborate on that?"

"To be honest, I try not to think too much about it. I guess you could say that I'm repressing those memories. For many years they haunted me, but once I went to live with the Brooke family, I decided to put the bad years behind me and not dwell on them. There's so much good in life, I'd rather keep my mind focused on the positive."

"Which is why you are such a refreshingly sweet and innocent person."

"Do you think so?"

"I do. Now, not to dwell too much on it, but if you wouldn't mind satisfying my curiosity—how was your childhood actually Dickensian? Were you ill-treated, beaten, starved?"

"At times, all of those things. I don't remember much of the first years, of course. The couple who wanted to adopt me, but who died in a car accident, are only the faintest whisper of memory. When I try to remember them, I do have a vague sense of love and warmth. After that I was shuffled through a succession of foster homes with varying degrees of comfort. Sometimes the foster parents were poor and just trying to bring in some extra income by taking on a child. I didn't really get the benefit of the payments in terms of good food or clothing. I wasn't included in the family. I felt more of a burden than any-thing else."

"Was there a particularly bad home or were they all pretty bad?"

"The worst was the Ralstons. That was the family I lived with for several years prior to the Brookes. They had two daughters and a mean little son, who had a perverse sadistic streak. The girls would exclude me from all their games and the son would tease me or hit me. One day I had had enough and I hit him back. He went off to his mother to tattle on me and was fake-crying so she locked me in a dark closet for the rest of the day. I was terrified."

"That must have been very traumatic," he observed sym-pathetically. "How old were you?"

"About ten. Mrs. Ralston really had it in for me. I don't know why such a person would take in foster children. She couldn't handle her own kids, let alone me. I think her husband was the altruistic one. He was kind to me when he was around, but he traveled a lot. She just seemed to resent my very existence and took every opportunity to let me know that I wasn't wanted by her or the other children. Mr. Ralston died when I was twelve and things took a terrible turn for the worst. I was put on restriction for any little thing—especially for the trumped-up complaints of the son."

"How were you restricted?"

"I wasn't allowed to go anywhere—even outside to play. Many times I had to skip dinner, and sometimes she would lock me again in that terrible closet."

"Then what happened?"

"Mrs. Ralston decided finally that she was sick of the very sight of me and that I wasn't worth the compensation she received as a foster parent. She began contacting girls' homes to take me. Thankfully, the social worker caught wind of it and moved me to the Brookes' home."

We arrived back to Carter Plantation. Mrs. Carter thanked Mr. Remington for the evening out, gave him a peck on the cheek, and excused herself to her rooms. Mr. Remington walked with me to my suite and casually leaned against the doorjamb as we concluded our conversation.

"And were you happy with the Brookes?"

"Very. They are amazing people and really included me as one of the family. The two oldest girls, Diane and Sharon, have become my closest friends, really sisters to me. I'm excited about being with them all over the holidays—but I am sorry I won't be able to see Cadence open her Christmas gifts."

He started, standing upright. "What the blazes do you mean? Why won't you?"

"Didn't Mrs. Carter tell you? I won't be here for Christmas. I leave tomorrow to stay with the Brookes."

"No! No one told me any such thing," he said, scowling. "How long will you be gone?"

"For Christmas week. I'll be back on New Year's Day."

"New Year's Eve," he corrected.

"Pardon?"

"I want you to return by New Year's Eve. Will you do that for me?"

"Yes, of course I will."

"Good. But what is Cadence supposed to do without you for Christmas?"

"She'll have her father, won't she? And her great-aunt. Plus Marta and Corinne will be on hand to help."

"So it's all arranged."

"Yes. Just as it was at Thanksgiving. My contract does entitle me to holidays off, you know."

"Your contract? Ah yes. I forget you are an employee. Why, then, take your Christmas holiday. But how will you get there?"

"I'll drive my Honda."

"Do you need any money?"

"No, thank you. I'm fine."

He opened his wallet anyway and counted out five one-hundred-dollar bills. "Here," he said, "take some cash, just in case."

"But you don't owe me anything."

"So what? Take it as a gift. A Christmas gift."

"You already gave me my Christmas gift—the camera."

"Right. But take this as well. You can call it a Christmas bonus."

I shook my head. "It's too much."

Considering for a moment, he put four bills back into his wallet and handed one to me. "Take this then, as a bonus. You're right, five is too much. If you have that, you may decide you don't need to return."

I smiled and accepted the hundred. "All right. Thank you very much. You're very kind."

"Wait a minute!" he exclaimed. "Maybe I shouldn't give you any bonus or you'll stay away too long. Give that back to me. I'll let you have it when you return."

"No, sir," I said with a laugh, hiding the bill behind my back. "I will not. I won't let you renege on a gift."

He grinned. "You little elf. Just promise me you'll be back for New Year's Eve."

"I promise."

"When do you leave?"

"Early tomorrow morning."

"So, this is good-bye then?"

"Good-bye for now."

"Good-bye doesn't seem adequate somehow."

"Merry Christmas, then?" I suggested, extending my hand.

He grasped my hand and then drew me to him.

"A mere handshake won't do," he said huskily. "Merry Christmas, my dear Jillian."

For a few sublime moments, he held me close to his heart.

15

I would hardly call my Christmas holiday a vacation in the traditional sense of the word. My time with the Brooke family was not restful—a holiday with eight children could never be that—but it was tremendous fun. Nearly as soon as the younger Brookes' excitement at my homecoming had subsided into a boisterous clamor, Mom Brooke had handed me an apron and marshaled me into joining the kitchen brigade of the older Brooke children, baking cookies and stirring fudge. Occasionally, Dad Brooke or the oldest brother, John, would check in on us to sample the wares, only to be shooed away.

Once we had put the younger children to bed, Sharon, Diane, and I helped Mom Brooke wrap all the presents—which, even with the Brookes' modest means and limit of three gifts per person, added up to quite a stash. We chatted and laughed as we worked to the merry strains of Christmas carols. After bombarding me with questions about my trip to England, Keswick Hall, and the film premier, they teased me about my quite evident crush on Ethan Remington. Sharon, Diane, and I talked and giggled late into the night, and I truly felt like I was one of the sisters.

At the Christmas Eve candlelight service, I said a special prayer of blessing for Mr. Remington, Cadence, and all the household back at Carter Plantation. I hoped they would like the gifts I had left under the giant tree in the great hall. The Brooke family certainly seemed pleased with the souvenirs I had brought back from England and which they opened gleefully with their other gifts in the chaos of Christmas morning.

Besides missing the Remingtons, one other thing clouded my holiday. The day after Christmas, as I was helping to collect discarded wrapping paper for the fire and straighten up the piles of opened gifts, Mom Brooke drew me aside.

"Jillian," she said gently, "there is something we thought you should know. We heard through some friends that your former foster mother, Mrs. Ralston, is in hospice care with pancreatic cancer. Apparently, she's not long for this world. They actually did not expect her to live until Christmas and certainly don't think she'll make it to the New Year."

"Oh my." That was all I could think to say. I frankly had tried to keep Mrs. Ralston out of my mind for the past several years. Now the images of her screaming at me, slapping me, or shoving me in a dark closet came flooding back. But somehow I felt detached from it all as though I were watching a film in which I was not an actor. I realized that her emotional hold, which had gripped me so long, had been broken by time and changing circumstances. She had reduced me to an unwanted, unloved person of no value, but since that time, I had known what it meant to be appreciated and even loved. I could actually feel pity for her now.

"I'm sorry to remind you of her, but I thought you'd want to know," Mom Brooke was saying in a soothing tone.

"No, that's all right. I appreciate it," I said. "What do you think I should do, Mom?"

"You don't have to do anything, honey. But if you could find it in your heart to forgive her, then do so for your sake as well as hers. And say a prayer for her as she passes on."

As she spoke, an idea came to my mind. "You know," I said slowly, "maybe I should go to visit her and try to make peace with her before she dies."

Mom Brooke gave a little gasp of surprise. "Why, Jillian, that would be really admirable of you, but are you sure you want to put yourself through that?"

I nodded. "I really don't want to see her, but if I don't, then I may always regret it. And what do I have to lose? She can't physically hurt me anymore, and I think I'm beyond her being able to control me emotionally. Who knows, she could be sorry now for how she treated me, and it would help her pass more peacefully to have some closure. I think maybe God is prompting me to at least try."

"Well, then, you should obey that prompting. Would you like any of us to come with you for moral support?"

"If you don't mind, that would be nice, but I should probably go in to talk to her by myself."

Since it was officially Boxing Day, a day for holiday visiting, we agreed not to delay and decided to drive over to the hospice center that very afternoon. The Brookes' oldest son, John, who served as an assistant pastor at a church in nearby Charlottesville, came with us and prayed aloud for me before I left the car. It comforted me to know that they were still praying for me as I nervously walked alone through the doors into that hushed domain of impending death.

I was surprised to see the facility cheerfully decorated for the holidays, but then I realized every effort would be made to provide comfort to the patients and their families. A gray-haired woman with a kind face welcomed me and asked whom I would like to visit.

"Mrs. Ralston," I said, holding up a small poinsettia, as if in explanation.

"How nice. Are you family?"

"No, but I was once her foster child."

"Well, I'm sure she'd be pleased to see you if she's awake. Since she's been here, her children haven't been able to come by very often. Now, she's fairly heavily drugged, so she may not be very responsive. But come this way."

I followed her to a dormitory-type room where curtains divided the beds into private compartments. A sweet sickly smell, which shall forever be associated in my mind with this solemn place, assaulted my senses. We passed several beds, where family and friends had gathered quietly around their ill loved ones, until we came to the bed of Mrs. Ralston. Her partition was void of visitors. She was utterly alone.

My nervousness dissipated into profound pity. She appeared little more than a skeleton. I could see some remnant of the stern visage of the woman who had once struck terror into my heart, but without any question, death had her in his dreadful grip.

She must have sensed my presence because she stirred and croaked, "Wa-ter."

I placed the poinsettia on her bed table and spied a bottle with a straw. Lifting her gently by the shoulders, I supported her while she took some sips.

She sighed and leaned back on her pillows. Examining me more closely, she asked, "Who are you?"

"I'm Jillian Dare. Several years ago, I lived with you as a foster child."

"Jillian Dare," she murmured. "I remember her. I never liked that girl. She was such a pitiful little brat."

"Mrs. Ralston," I said, "I am Jillian."

"You, Jillian Dare! You've haunted me these past years and here you are haunting me again. Why?"

"I heard that you were ill and I've come to see you to tell you that I'm sorry for whatever I did to make you unhappy or dislike me. But that was a long time ago. I was only a child, and I'm all grown up now. I hope you can forgive me. I have forgiven you, Mrs. Ralston. I came to say good-bye and to part in peace."

Compassion swept over me. As I spoke those words, I

knew that I truly had forgiven her. I covered her hand with my own, but she quickly drew hers back and turned her face to the wall.

"I am dying," she muttered. "I must rest. Go away."

"I know you are dying, Mrs. Ralston, and I am truly sorry you are suffering. I had hoped that we could be reconciled. You can turn away from me, but you can't turn away from God. I will pray that you will make your peace with him."

She emitted a little moan but made no other response. I stood for a few moments longer and then stole sadly away. Her eternal destiny was in God's merciful hands. I prayed for her to find peace in him, and as I did, I sensed his peace settle softly in my own heart. I had wished for a better outcome but felt assured I had done what God required of me.

After that sad venture, my week in the valley sped by quickly. But despite how loved and at home I felt with the Brookes, my heart longed to be back to my new home and to Ethan Remington.

❧

When I arrived at Carter Plantation the afternoon of New Year's Eve, Mr. Remington himself opened the door to greet me. His dark brown eyes brightened with genuine pleasure, and he smiled magnanimously.

"Jillian! Welcome home! I missed you."

My breath caught in my throat. Even he considered Carter Plantation to be my home now.

I finally blurted out, "I missed you too."

"I'm so glad you're back. I was worried you might not return for New Year's Eve."

"I promised I would, didn't I? Did you have a nice Christmas?"

"Yes, except for your absence. Here I'd like to show you something." He took my hand and led me to his study, where he gestured to the wall. Mounted in a prominent position hung two of my gifts to him: one, a montage of photos I had taken of him and Cadence; the other, my photograph of Keswick Hall seeming to float above the lake at sunset.

"You see?" he said. "Already on display. And this one"—he indicated a third framed photo of Carter Plantation in its autumnal splendor—"I plan to hang in my study in Keswick Hall. That way no matter which home I'm in, I can enjoy the other."

"That's great! It's just what I hoped you would do! So you like them?"

"Of course, I do," he said, smiling. "Thank you very much. They are lovely pictures."

"I'm so glad you think so, and thank *you* for the camera."

"You're most welcome. Now then," he said, clasping his hands together. "The reason I wanted you back for tonight is that I have made reservations for a New Year's Eve dinner at the Inn at Little Washington."

"Okay." I swallowed my disappointment. "I'd be happy to take care of Cadence tonight."

He chuckled. "Oh no, you won't. Cadence will be safely

tucked in bed, and Aunt Elise will keep an eye on her. I would like for you to go to dinner with me."

"Me?" I fairly squeaked. I had never even dared to dream about going to such an expensive and exclusive restaurant.

"Yes." He smiled. "Will you?"

I was flustered but managed to say, "Sure. I'd love to."

"Good. Now I'll let you go unpack and dress. We'll leave at half past seven." He hesitated and then added mildly, "By the way, would you mind terribly wearing your hair down tonight? You have such gorgeous hair, Jillian."

He admired my hair? I gulped. "Okay, sure. Um . . . what's the suggested attire for tonight?"

"Coat and tie required. You could wear that fetching black dress I saw you in at the premier party."

Dumfounded, I nodded. How had he noticed *my* dress among the beautiful gowns of all those glittering movie stars?

"Excellent." He smiled happily. "Half past seven then. I'll drive the Lamborghini to the front door to pick you up."

I found myself bewildered by the unfolding events. Bewildered but excited. To be treated to dinner by Ethan Remington as a date, as an equal, exceeded all my hopes.

Perhaps the rumors of a pending marriage with Brittany Graham were only rumors after all.

※

That evening I wondered if Cinderella had felt like I did. I was actually on a date with my Prince Charming, Ethan

Remington. And not just any date. We were celebrating New Year's Eve together at the five-star Inn at Little Washington. While we dined on gourmet fare, a string quartet serenaded us with Bach, Mozart, and Handel.

Ethan regaled me with descriptions of his Christmas and how Cadence had danced with excitement at the sight of the lighted tree surrounded with gifts. He added with a wry smile that she had been more entertained by unwrapping her gifts than by the gifts themselves—excepting my little lamb, of course, which she absolutely adored. He then encouraged me to share about my holiday with the Brooke family.

"So was it a good Christmas for you?" he asked.

"Yes, it was."

"I'm glad." He studied me for a moment. "But I think there's something bothering you. You look a bit sad. Did anything unpleasant happen while you were there?"

Sometimes it seemed as if he could read my mind. "Why, yes, as a matter of fact. Something did happen that was both sad and unpleasant."

"Would you like to tell me about it?"

I shared the entire story of my hospice visit with Mrs. Ralston.

Mr. Remington reached across the table and took my hand. "I'm sorry, Jillian. That is sad. But you were very brave and I'm proud of you for trying. I just don't know how you found the courage to face her, and how you could forgive her after the way she treated you."

"I don't know myself. Maybe it was the grace of God. I didn't think I could ever forgive her, but then when I saw her, all of a sudden, I could." I added, "I'm sure the Brookes were praying for me."

"Maybe they should pray for me," he said thoughtfully. "There are some people I don't think I can ever forgive."

"In your own strength, you can't, but if you ask for God's help, I'm sure he would give it to you."

"I can almost believe it when I gaze at your sweet face. You, Jillian, are my good angel." He sighed. "But if you knew what I've suffered . . ."

He didn't finish his thought but smiled ruefully. "Well, now, it's time for me to get the check." He signaled the waiter. "I'd rather not be driving these back country roads after midnight with a lot of drunk drivers about and with snow in the forecast. Besides, I have a bottle of sparkling cider chilling for us at home."

"Cider?"

"Yes. I remembered you are underage for champagne here in Virginia, and I don't want to compromise you. So, we'll see the New Year in with sparkling cider."

On the ride home, he suddenly glanced at me and, smiling, asked, "Jillian, what would you think if I were to tell you that I hope to remarry as soon as possible?"

I literally felt sick to my stomach. The tabloids had been right after all. He must have taken me out to dinner to soften the blow of my having to find new employment.

"Jillian?"

"I'm sorry. I suppose congratulations are in order, but I can't help being selfish. I was just thinking that if you are to marry, then that will change my circumstances."

"Why, yes, it would indeed."

I forced myself to continue. "And you would need to find a new nanny for Cadence."

"Would I?" he asked with some surprise.

"Well, yes. I think so."

"I thought you'd want to continue to care for Cadence, but if not, that's all right. We can hire another nanny if you like."

I sat in shocked silence for the remainder of the ride home. A sudden snow squall furiously blew about, requiring Mr. Remington's total concentration to maintain control of the car. Perhaps, then, my silence had gone unheeded. The more I considered Mr. Remington's revelation, the more I struggled to fight back the hot tears pricking the back of my eyes.

When we had returned to the house, I began to thank Mr. Remington for the lovely dinner, trying to maintain some dignity long enough to retreat to my suite. But he would not let me leave. He insisted that we go to the family room, where a fire and the sparkling cider awaited our New Year's celebration.

I hardly felt like celebrating.

"Jillian," he said, looking at me with concern. "Sit down here beside me on the couch. There now. Whatever is the matter?"

"How can you not know?" I asked, and to my dismay, I lost all decorum and burst into tears.

"What is it? What's wrong?"

I shook my head and sobbed.

"My darling, whatever is the matter?" He took me in his arms with such tenderness that I wept all the more.

"You said you plan to be married soon!" I interspersed my words with wrenching sobs. "I know Brittany will not want me around. And I will have to go. How can I stand it? Do you think that just because I'm a young, ordinary girl that I don't have any feelings? I do! You have made me love you. I can't help it. There, I've said it now. I love you! She does not, and I know you don't love her either. It doesn't matter how beautiful or talented she is. She will never love you the way I do. If I were beautiful like she is, I would make it as hard for you to leave me as it is for me to leave you!"

"Whatever are you talking about? Who said anything about you leaving me? Me marry Brittany Graham? Where on earth did you get such a ridiculous idea?"

"The tabloids, Karla, Corinne, they all said . . ."

"Hush! What do tabloids know? I definitely don't love Brittany, and she doesn't love me. You're absolutely right about that. All that fuss was merely a publicity stunt to promote the film. I never supposed you would be taken in by it."

"But you said in the car that you plan to marry."

"I do hope to."

"But whom?"

"Why, you, dear girl, of course! I wish to marry you!" He

stroked my hair and murmured, "I love you, Jillian, more than I have ever loved any other woman. And you just said you love me. How splendid it is to hear you say that! We are kindred spirits, darling, aren't we? It's as if our hearts and souls are knitted together."

I shoved him away. "Don't tease me! It's mean of you."

He looked taken aback. "I'm not teasing, Jillian. How could you think that? I couldn't be more perfectly serious."

Suddenly, to my utter astonishment, he dropped to one knee before me. I could find no mockery in his demeanor. "Jillian, my darling," he said with complete sincerity, "will you do me the honor of becoming my wife? Will you marry me?"

The situation wavered on the surreal. "You're not joking?" I asked slowly. "This is for real?"

"Nothing could be more real. Here, I'll prove it." Putting his hand in his pocket, he pulled out a small jewelry box, which he sprang open to reveal a brilliant diamond. "You see, I hoped you would say yes, so I went ahead and purchased a ring. Now please, Jillian, will you marry me?"

I stared incredulously at the gleaming ring. "Oh my! It is for real—but I still can't believe it."

He smiled. "Believe it. And please say yes."

"Yes!" I cried, throwing my arms around his neck. "Yes, Ethan, yes, I will!"

We both laughed and hugged each other tightly. He kissed me then, gently at first and then more urgently. I melted into his kisses and embrace. We parted reluctantly only when we heard the grandfather clock chime twelve.

"It's midnight," he said, handing me a glass of sparkling cider and holding his own aloft. "To us! May we be blessed with a long and happy marriage."

"To us!" I repeated, scarcely able to comprehend the wonderful turn of events. I had entered this room with all my dreams dashed, and now he had marvelously fulfilled them beyond my wildest expectations.

"Happy New Year, darling."

"Happy New Year, Ethan."

We clinked our glasses together, reveling in the warmth of our mutual joy. But outside, the howling wind whipped up the snow into a frenzy of blinding swirls.

16

When I awoke the next morning, a sparkling cloak of snow had covered over the blight of barren winter, transforming the garden and fields beyond into a dazzling, wintry fairyland.

Nature itself reflected my joy.

I could scarcely believe what had happened to me. Ethan Remington had said he loved me and had asked me to be his wife! For a few moments, I questioned if I had imagined everything, but when I stared down at the diamond ring winking on my finger, I knew it was indeed true.

Ethan Remington loved *me*!

I smiled at my reflection as I dressed for breakfast. To my amazement, the girl in the mirror, with her long golden-brown hair and smiling, aquamarine eyes, actually looked pretty.

I, Jillian Virginia Dare, am loved!

Despite the assurance of the engagement ring I wore, I had some qualms on entering the dining room and wondered how I would be greeted. Ethan had urged me to sleep in as late as I desired, promising to take care of Cadence himself, and they were both still at breakfast with Mrs. Carter when I stood tentatively in the doorway.

As soon as he saw me, Ethan sprang to his feet and rushed over to embrace me. My qualms evaporated in his arms.

"Good morning, my darling! Happy New Year! Isn't it a glorious day?" He held me at arm's length, eagerly devouring me with his eyes. "And don't you look beautiful this morning!"

I laughed. "You look pretty good yourself." Indeed, he positively glowed with happiness.

"Here, come be seated," he said, withdrawing the chair next to his own. "Marta has prepared a fabulous New Year's brunch for us here on the sideboard. What do you fancy? I'll serve you myself."

I peered over at the buffet as I sat down. "I'll have some creamed chipped beef on biscuits, please."

"Chipped beef it is!" he declared merrily. "Cadence has been enjoying her chipped beef as well."

The baby smiled at hearing her name, through globs of white sauce smeared on her cheeks.

I returned her smile and then noticed Mrs. Carter. She was not smiling but staring down at her plate.

"Good morning, Mrs. Carter," I said. "Happy New Year."

She glanced up. "Happy New Year," she replied quietly.

Ethan placed a china plate of steaming chipped beef and a small crystal bowl of fresh fruit in front of me. "There you are. And here's some orange juice and the coffee's on the table."

"Thank you. This looks fantastic."

He resumed his seat and spread his napkin over his lap. "Well, now. Just before you came in, Jillian, I was telling Aunt Elise our good news."

Mrs. Carter glanced up again and mustered a tight smile. "Congratulations."

"Thank you," I said slowly.

A few moments of awkward silence ensued when suddenly Mrs. Carter blurted out, "I'm sorry, but I am still in shock. Ethan, are you sure this is a good idea? What will the neighbors think? I adore Jillian too, but she is our nanny, you know. It's hardly appropriate. And she's so much younger than you are. Can you imagine the gossip columns getting a hold of this?"

I felt deflated. I had thought that Mrs. Carter really liked me and mistakenly believed she would be pleased for Cadence to have me become her mother.

Ethan seemed unperturbed. "If we are prudent, the gossip columns needn't know about it, Auntie, nor should the neighbors. I plan to keep our engagement quiet until the wedding."

"And when will that be? When can that be? You still—"

"Four months," he interrupted, raising his hand in a halting gesture. "In four months, all will be finalized and we can be married." He gave me a tender look. "What do you say to a May wedding, Jillian? We could have an intimate garden reception right here. The azaleas will be blooming, and it will be lovely."

"May would be perfect. I've always thought that May is one of the prettiest months of the year."

"But you're so young, Jillian," Mrs. Carter protested. "You're only twenty. You're practically a child."

"I'll be twenty-one by May, and legally I'm old enough to be married right now," I said, somewhat defensively. Mrs. Carter's lack of approval disappointed me deeply.

"When's your birthday, darling?" Ethan asked gently.

"April tenth."

"I forget you are so young. But it doesn't matter anyway." He turned to his aunt and declared like a man used to wielding authority, "I love Jillian, Aunt Elise, and she loves me. And we will be married in May. We will have a small, private wedding right here at Carter Plantation, and we will be quiet about it until the time is right. And that is that. Now then, Jillian?"

"Yes?"

"I'm sorry to say that I must return to England on the fourth. I'd like you to come with me."

"Okay, sure. But Cadence . . ."

"After what happened on our last trip, I will not be taking Cadence this time. I'll call the Nanny Brigade tomorrow and arrange for a temp. We'll only be gone for a few days."

Mrs. Carter's frown did not escape Ethan's notice.

"What is it now, Aunt Elise?"

"Ethan, I know you are used to doing things your own way, and thankfully I am not around to see it most of the time. But even though this house belongs to you now, I cannot stand by and watch you drag this young girl into immoral behavior right here under my roof. And to travel abroad with her! Your uncle would be rolling over in his grave, as would your parents, if they knew."

Ethan smiled indulgently. "Don't worry, Auntie. I am not dragging her into immoral behavior. We are not sleeping together if you're concerned about that. And we won't over in England either—not until we're married, anyway. I promise. No one will be rolling over in their graves."

Mrs. Carter sighed with undisguised relief. "I'm so glad to hear that. I may be old-fashioned, but I was really concerned that with your having been married before and all your experience, and her being such an innocent little thing . . . Oh, I'm sorry, Ethan. I shouldn't have misjudged you."

He patted her hand. "No, you were right to question my intentions. The truth is that most men don't have good ones. But in this case"—he smiled at me—"in this case, Jillian is my good angel. She is so sweet and so pure that I must stay on the straight and narrow with her. Don't you worry on that account."

"Ethan," I spoke up. "Perhaps it would be best for me to stay at home with Cadence."

"But I want you with me. I want you both with me, actually, but I don't think this is a good time to take her back to England. I don't like being away from either of you."

"And we don't like being away from you either. But think of the baby. She doesn't understand, and it would be very hard on her to have us both gone."

"You're right, of course. But I don't want you to consider yourself as her nanny any longer. You mentioned something about that last night. I can hire someone else if you prefer."

"No, there is no need for that. Last night I misunderstood you. Until we are married, I really prefer to continue to serve as Cadence's nanny. After that, I hope you will allow me to be her mother."

Ethan smiled. "Some people may get it into their heads that I'm marrying you just so Cadence will have a mother. She does need a mother, and you will make her a fine one. But that is not why I want to marry you. I need you for my wife."

A sudden clattering startled all three of us. Cadence had pushed her silver bowl onto the floor. Instinctively, I rose.

"No, I'll get it." Ethan stood and motioned for me to stay seated. "You finish your breakfast. I'll take Cadence into the kitchen to clean her up."

When they had left and I resumed eating, Mrs. Carter leaned toward me.

"Jillian, I know you probably think that I'm a terrible old busybody, but you must believe that I'm trying to look out for you. I think of you as practically a member of the family, and neither you nor Ethan has a mother or father to guide you. That's why I must tell you that you can't be too careful. Ethan may have all the best intentions toward you, but you know as well as I how impetuous and passionate he can be. Even though you are engaged, you must avoid being alone with him. Otherwise, his passions may get the better of you both. And even if nothing happens, you need to be careful of not giving the appearance of wrongdoing. Do you understand what I'm trying to say?"

"Yes, ma'am. I do. I'll be careful and I'll do as you say."

"That's a good girl. At least you have some common sense. Maybe you will be good for Ethan."

"I think I am," I said stiffly.

"Yes, of course you are, my dear. I'm sorry to be such a stick-in-the-mud. I know Ethan is fond of you, and he seems much happier since you've come here. But there is so much you don't know about each other—that you don't know about him. Has he told you about—"

"About how much I love you?" Ethan asked as he carried a freshly scrubbed Cadence back into the dining room and bent down to kiss me on the cheek. "I absolutely adore you. Now, are you finished eating? What would you say to a sleigh ride? You too, Auntie. I've asked Jack to hitch up Daystar. Everybody, let's get suited up. We're about to go dashing through the snow!"

What could be more delightful than being snowed in with Ethan Remington? Taking a sleigh ride had been merely an unrealized fantasy of mine until this bright New Year's Day. And we actually played in the snow: sledding down the rolling hills of Carter Plantation, sculpting an enormous snowman, and hurling snowballs with which Ethan, in a quite gentlemanly fashion, just avoided hitting me.

Later, we flopped down in easy chairs and sipped hot chocolate laden with marshmallows, while toasting our feet in front of the fire. We talked and laughed and talked some more. In the evening, we watched football, snuggling together on the couch.

We reveled in each other's companionship.

The next four months of engagement passed by in a whirl of similarly pleasant outings and cozy domestic moments. Ethan kept his promise of maintaining proper decorum with me both in public and in private. He also made certain that Cadence, as well as his aunt Elise, were included in our intimate circle. I felt that I had truly become part of my own little family unit.

At last, I really belonged to someone. I belonged to Ethan Remington and he belonged to me. I could barely contain my joy, and Ethan brimmed with exuberance and his own happiness.

It never occurred to me then that I had neglected to ask God what his will for me was, or that I had wholeheartedly transferred my allegiance and adoration from my Creator to one of his creatures. It didn't occur to me then, but it became starkly clear to me later. Quite gradually and without my actual awareness, Ethan Remington had not only stolen my heart, he had become my first—my only—love.

And that was to have perilous consequences.

17

*S*pring graced the Virginia countryside with bright green meadows, budding trees, and the pink and white lace of dogwoods. She decked her gardens with crocuses, daffodils, forsythia, and tulips. When the azaleas were close to bursting forth in a profusion of lavender and fuchsia blossoms, I knew my wedding day was fast approaching.

Ethan had desired an intimate wedding and reception at Carter Plantation with just the household and Calvin Cole in attendance. Since I am an introvert and averse to being the center of attention, this desire pleased me as well. My only regret was not including the Brooke family, particularly my friends Sharon and Diane; but Ethan promised we would invite the entire family for a weekend stay once we had returned from our honeymoon cruise of the Greek Islands.

Over the course of our engagement, Ethan had to travel back and forth several times to the UK on business, but we had agreed I would stay at home to care for Cadence. However, just before the wedding, Ethan hired a temporary nanny and asked me to accompany him to London. He had taken a particular fancy to the idea that I should have my wedding gown and veil created by the same designer's house who had made his mother's, and I wanted to indulge this desire of his. Together we had selected a simple design and placed the order, but I needed to have a final fitting in person.

Ethan planned to conduct all of his business and our shopping in the city of London, and since he did not wish for us to stay out at Keswick Hall, he secured a suite of connecting rooms for us at the Ritz Hotel in Mayfair. Calvin Cole accompanied us on this trip, serving as our unofficial chaperone.

Although Ethan had taken pains to keep our engagement quiet in the United States, someone must have tipped off the paparazzi about our stay at the Ritz. On our second day in London, the tabloid headlines screamed, "The Producer and the Nanny!" and "Remington Steals Nanny's Heart!" Underneath was a fuzzy photo, probably taken on a cell phone, of the two of us emerging from a taxi.

I was horrified. Ethan philosophically observed that he was grateful I had not traveled with him on previous occasions. In any case, the tabloids had gotten it right this time, and we would be married soon enough.

On the morning of the appointment for my fitting, Ethan had taken me shopping in Oxford Street for my trousseau. I still did not enjoy shopping, but Ethan evidently did—at least he seemed eager for me to have a wardrobe befitting a wealthy executive and producer's wife. After arranging to have the new clothes shipped back to Virginia, Ethan dropped me off at the bridal shop for my fitting, promising to return in one hour.

"I have some business to attend to with Calvin, and then everything will be set for the wedding," Ethan said. "While you're here, I'd like for you to try on some different veils with your gown, all right?"

"But we talked about this before," I protested. "I like the very simple fingertip veil."

"Jillian, this shop has reams of beautiful handmade Belgian lace veils. Please, at least look at some of them. And you are welcome to indulge yourself in some lovely lace lingerie too."

I gave him a wry smile. "You mean, indulge you."

He grinned and kissed me. "That's right, indulge me. Buy some pretty things. Enjoy yourself, though. I'll be back as soon as I can."

"Okay."

Ethan gave the salesgirl some similar instructions and then left me to be tugged and fussed over by the seamstress, a small Asian woman, who with her mouthful of pins could only grunt instructions.

I loved my gown, a creamy silk, cut on the bias that hugged

my narrow waist and flared to the floor. It was simple and elegant, which I hoped reflected me. The fitting, however, took much longer than I had expected. Even though we had sent over my measurements beforehand, the seamstress needed to take up the gown quite a bit in length and along the seams.

While I stood, enduring the pushing and pulling of the fitting, the salesgirl dutifully brought over pieces of lacey lingerie for me to peruse, followed by a parade of veils.

At last, I found one that I especially liked. With its thin but exquisite lace border, it complemented the gown in simplicity and elegance.

"This one!" I cried as she gently placed it over my head and pinned it to my hair.

"It's perfect," she concurred.

At that moment, the bell over the shop door jangled and Ethan and Calvin hurried in. An indistinct babble of voices floated behind them as they opened the door and then hushed as the door closed.

"Don't come in here now, sir!" warned the seamstress. "It's bad luck to see the bride before the wedding day."

Ethan stopped short on the edge of the dressing room. I could see his face reflected in the mirror in front of me, but I couldn't make out how to read his expression. Wasn't he pleased? Why was he suddenly glowering?

"What do you think of this veil, Ethan?" I asked almost shyly.

"It's beautiful. You're beautiful!" He clutched his head as if in agony. "Oh—this is bloody awful!"

I turned around. "Ethan, what's wrong? What is the matter?"

Calvin had come to his side and gripped his arm. "You have to tell her, Ethan."

Ethan groaned.

"What is it? What's wrong?" I asked again, an unreasonable fear seizing me.

"You can't be married," Calvin said heavily. "At least not yet. There's been an unforeseen difficulty."

"Difficulty? What do you mean? Ethan, what is he talking about?"

"Jillian." Ethan's face was deathly pale. "He's right. We must postpone the wedding. Take the gown off and get dressed. I'll explain it to you in private."

For a moment I just stood there. I couldn't believe what I was hearing. What could be so terribly wrong?

The shop doorbell jangled, and the babble of voices grew louder.

"Ethan!" a shrill voice called. "Ethan!"

A tall, statuesque woman, surrounded by a group of photographers and reporters, charged into the shop. Bulbs popped in blinding flashes, but I could not take my eyes off the woman. She had the perfected beauty of a fashion model. I didn't recognize her, and yet I sensed I had seen her before. She stared back at me.

And then I suddenly knew her.

She is the Woman in White!

"Crystal, what are you doing here?" Ethan asked.

"So, this is your little nanny-whore!" she sneered. "You want to marry this little slut?"

"Crystal, please leave." Ethan turned on the paparazzi. "You people, get out! Now!" he demanded. "This is a private shop. Get out or I'll call the coppers!"

With a murmur, the crowd began turning to leave the shop. Suddenly, the woman gave a savage cry and dove at me, ripping the veil from my hair and clawing at me.

I staggered back and covered my face with my hands. Ethan grabbed the fury's arms, and she turned her attack on him, beating him, scratching him in a wild frenzy. Calvin intervened, pinning her hands down as she struggled. The photographers snapped away, bulbs flashing, everyone shouting.

A bobby off the street muscled his way through the throng and blew his whistle to restore some semblance of order. The seamstress must have called the police as the bobby soon had several officers backing him up.

I stood quietly, still wearing my wedding gown, and watched as the officers led away the ranting woman to a squad car, the paparazzi having a field day taking pictures. Ethan dabbed his handkerchief at the bleeding scratches on his face while Calvin tried to calm the nearly hysterical salesgirl.

Ethan saw me then and took me in his arms. "Are you all right, darling? She didn't hurt you, did she?"

She had yanked out some of my hair, but I shook my head. "I'm all right," I said.

"Thank God!" He pulled me closer.

"But you! You're bleeding."

"It's nothing, just some scratches."

I heard then the din of the reporters but couldn't make any sense of their words.

"Mr. Remington, obviously Crystal Carter won't let you go without a fight!"

"Mr. Remington, how can you marry your nanny now?"

"Mr. Remington, did you know Crystal would fight for you?"

"Mr. Remington, who will win custody of your baby?"

"Mr. Remington . . ."

The officers ordered the reporters out of the store. By then, newsmen with video cameras had gathered on the sidewalk, jostling for a prime shot for the evening news. Inside, the policemen began to interview the witnesses and take notes. One asked me to recount what I had seen and heard. I answered in a daze.

"May I change out of this gown, please?" I finally asked.

The policeman looked embarrassed at my predicament. "Of course, Miss."

He shooed everyone but the salesgirl out of the dressing area. She helped to slip the gown over my head, and her hands trembled as she hung it up.

"My word," she said. "I don't believe it. What a temper she has! Good grief, she was scary! And the way she flew at you. You poor thing! Are you all right?"

"Who is she?" I asked, pulling my dress back on over my slip.

"You didn't recognize her?"

"No. Who is she?"

"That was Crystal Carter, of course. She's a bit of a celebrity here in London. She's a singer and dancer. And actress—both film and stage. Right now she's in that Andrew Lloyd Webber musical in the West End. Um . . . what's it called?"

"*The Woman in White*?"

"That's right. That's the one."

"But who is she to Mr. Remington?"

"Why, don't you know? She's his wife."

"His . . . wife?"

"Well, yes. At least she was. They have been separated for a long time. I assumed they were divorced since he's planning to marry you now. But after what just happened . . ."

I slumped down in the middle of the floor.

"Miss? Miss? Are you all right?"

With one blow, my entire life had been keeled over like a swamped ship. If I had been struck dead at that moment, I would have counted it bliss.

No, I was not all right, not at all. And I could not imagine how I ever would be again.

18

A knock on the door roused me. The salesgirl opened it to Ethan. Spying me crumpled on the floor, he rushed over and pulled me up.

"Jillian, are you all right? I ordered a taxi brought around to the back door. We'll go out that way to escape the paparazzi. Got your coat and handbag? Okay, let's go." He pulled me along by my hand, and I blindly followed.

"Sorry, Miss," he said to the salesgirl. "I apologize for the disruption. Please hold on to that gown and bill any damages to my account. Thank you for your assistance. Oh—and the police would like to get a statement from you."

I can dimly remember ducking into the taxi and riding back to the Ritz. Ethan and Calvin spoke in hurried, hushed tones as though we were in a limousine en route to a funeral. When we returned to our suite, I excused myself to my room. After shutting the door behind me, I threw myself prone onto my bed.

I expected the floodgates to open but they did not. Strangely, no tears came. Perhaps I was in shock. I certainly felt emotionally shocked. *Mr. Remington's wife is not dead! She is very much alive. She, Crystal Carter, is the malicious CC! Our wedding must be postponed, perhaps forever. Evidently, CC does not want to divorce Ethan. What has happened? What am I to do? What should I do? What can I do?*

I felt completely helpless and unable to think straight. My thoughts whirled around in my head, and I was incapable of reining them in. Suddenly in my agony, I cried out to God. "Help me please! Have mercy on me! Show me what to do!"

I did not move from the bed until the day dwindled and I could hear room service delivering a tea cart to the outer lounge area. Not having eaten since breakfast, I felt weak and exhausted from the lack of food as well as the emotional toll exacted by the day's events. I decided in the short term, I should get something to eat. Perhaps then I could think more clearly.

I opened the door and nearly fell over something blocking the doorway. Ethan had pulled a chair across the opening where he sat, like a watchdog on guard duty. At my stumble, he reached out and caught me in his arms.

"There you are at last!" he said. "I've been waiting for you all afternoon. You were so quiet in there, I was really beginning to be concerned. If you had not come out in just a few more minutes, I may have kicked the door down. Are you all right, darling? Can I get you anything?"

"I think I should have something to eat," I said.

He released me. "We have some sandwiches here. Will that be enough? If not, I can order something else for you. Here, come sit on the sofa and I'll bring it to you. Tell me what you fancy."

"Tea and sandwiches are fine. I'm not that hungry."

He fussed over me, making sure that I was well provided for. When he seemed satisfied I was sufficiently fortified, he began to talk.

"Jillian, I am so sorry things happened the way they did today. You must be in complete shock."

"You lied to me, Ethan."

"No, I did not."

"Then you didn't tell me the whole truth. You deliberately deceived me."

"I confess I withheld some of the truth. I meant to tell you all and shall. I'm so sorry to have hurt you this way."

"I thought your wife was dead!"

"Dead! Where did you get that idea? I never told you that!"

I thought hard about this. In truth, I had been thinking of it most of the afternoon. I couldn't recall him ever saying she was dead or much about her at all. He had once said that he had been abandoned by all he had loved. He had spoken of his parents who had died, and so I wrongly concluded his wife had died as well.

"I could swear Mrs. Carter said she had died."

"Aunt Elise knows Crystal is quite alive, so I doubt very much she would say that. Did she use the actual words 'died' or 'passed away'?"

I then recalled the conversation. "She said something about Mrs. Remington no longer being with us." My voice dropped to a whisper. "I thought she meant . . ."

"I'm so sorry, Jillian."

"But you—I remember now saying something to you about your wife having passed on and you said yes, she had."

"She had certainly moved on," he said bitterly. "But no, I did not mean to lead you to believe she had passed *away*. I'm sorry for the terrible misunderstanding."

"Are you divorced then?"

"Not yet. We were supposed to sign the final papers today. But at the solicitors' office this afternoon, Crystal suddenly changed her mind and refused to sign. I don't know why. Maybe she had seen one of those tabloid articles about us, and she felt threatened. She also said she would sue for custody of Cadence, which is an outrage since she is clearly over the edge and abandoned us. Anyway, she was in high dudgeon and must have followed us over to the dress shop, where she unleashed her fury on you. I'm so sorry to have exposed you to her. I did all I could to keep her away. In any case, it should all go against her in any custody case she tries to bring up."

"Ethan, you are a married man! You have a wife still living.

Why didn't you tell me about her? Why did you propose to me when you weren't free to do so?"

He took my hands in his. "Jillian, I am so sorry. I meant to tell you today after the papers were signed. I never meant to hurt you like this. Will you forgive me?"

His dark eyes were filled with remorse and pain. I had to forgive him.

I did.

"Yes, I forgive you," I said. "But that doesn't make it right. We shouldn't have gotten involved while you were still legally bound to her. It may still be possible for your marriage to be reconciled. Especially now, if that's what your wife wants."

He snorted a harsh laugh. "Did you see her today? *My wife?* Have you forgotten that she has tried to kill me at least twice? In attacking me, she almost succeeded in killing our daughter—her own child—and you too, I might add. You call that a *wife?* *A mother?* The woman is certifiably mad."

"Then she deserves your compassion. She can't help it if she's mentally ill. Didn't you promise to love her in sickness and in health? Aren't there medications that can help her?"

"Perhaps. If she would agree to take them. I have paid for her treatment by nearly a dozen mental health professionals in one year alone. Many of them disagreed on her diagnosis. A few even thought she was cunningly acting out the symptoms of paranoia and bipolarity for attention. She is an actress, you know. But then, I have to wonder—isn't it just a little bit crazy to act crazy? In any case, I was more than willing to get any possible help for her. I tried to, but there's a catch-22 to it all. If the patient doesn't want the help, you can rarely force it on them. And what person who has gone crackers has enough awareness and sense of reality to ask for help? You see what I mean?"

I nodded.

"If we could prove she was the one who set the fire and put the knife in my tire, we might be able to have her committed, based on her being a threat to others. But even then, she could probably check herself out of the mental health clinic after a few days. We've been through that cycle before, and then I've had to deal with her paranoid anger at my having committed her in the first place."

He studied me for a few minutes. "Do you know something? You are remarkable. You are genuinely concerned for her, aren't you?"

"Why, yes. I do feel sorry for her and wish she could get help. Especially before she tries to hurt someone else. And Ethan, I'm not sure I agree that her mental illness is grounds for you to divorce her."

He shook his head grimly. "Grounds? What about adultery and abandonment? Would that be grounds enough for you? Let me tell you my sad, sad story, Jillian, and perhaps you will understand how it's quite impossible for our marriage to be reconciled."

"All right. Tell me. I'm listening."

"Right. Here it is: the sad saga of Ethan Remington and Crystal Carter." He took a deep breath. "The first time I saw Crystal, she was a dancer in a musical in the West End. She was relatively unknown—her name was Crystal Smith then—but she was stunningly beautiful and incredibly sexy with those long, shapely legs of hers. And she was a genuinely talented dancer and singer.

"I was instantly smitten, and as soon as the show was over, I went backstage to meet her. She knew me by name— RemTel had taken off by then and I had already produced a couple of films. I was casting for a new film at the time and thought she would be perfect for the part. You could say I was the one to 'discover' her.

"She feigned an attachment to me, and before I had time to learn much about her other than her physical attributes, I found myself married to her and she was starring in my new film. She took my mother's family name of Carter, and Crystal Carter's star was born."

He sighed. "We had barely returned from our honeymoon when I discovered the character of the woman I had so impetuously and foolishly married. I made a surprise visit to the set. She was madly making out with her costar—off camera. He was at least ashamed to be caught—she merely laughed!

"I clearly understood then that she had only married me for my wealth and my influence. I was such a fool. She continued to treat me with utter contempt, having numerous liaisons, all the while freely spending my money. This went on for four miserable years. I probably should have annulled the marriage after that first week on the film set, but I am not a quitter, Jillian. Even when I knew she was being unfaithful and I had ample grounds for divorce, I tried to make it work."

I reached out and took his hand. "I'm sorry. You must have felt so betrayed and rejected."

"I could have borne my rejection. I did bear it, but then she became pregnant with Cadence, and that forced the issue for me. She actually wanted to have an abortion. She did not want to be pregnant and 'ruin' her career. Somehow, I convinced her to go through with the pregnancy. I was thrilled about the baby, even though I didn't know for certain if she were mine or someone else's until after she was born and she was tested."

"Is she yours?"

"Yes, thankfully she is. I think though that even if she weren't, I would still claim her as my own. I suggested the name of Cadence to evoke Crystal's singing and dancing and with the hope that she would bond with her. But Crystal wanted nothing to do with her. She refused to nurse her because it would 'ruin her figure.' She had to be forced to hold her in the hospital, and once she was home, she gave up all caretaking duties to Mrs. Poole."

"Postpartum depression?"

"I suppose so. When the baby was three weeks old, Crystal walked out and never returned. So she left us, quite literally."

"She left her baby?"

"Yes. Absolutely abandoned her."

Now that struck a chord. I had always wondered why my mother abandoned me as a baby. But I always supposed she had been driven by desperate measures. Perhaps she had even been an unwed college student who couldn't face her parents. The possibility that I could have simply not been wanted—that my mother had the means to care for me but was too self-centered to do so—had not occurred to me before. I shoved the thought out of my mind and considered only Cadence's rejection. How could anyone leave such a precious baby? Crystal had to be insane. Insane or incredibly selfish.

"I'm sorry," I said again, squeezing his hand in mine. "What did you do?"

"I tried to get her to come home. I coaxed, I begged, I pleaded, and tried all manner of bribes. I paid for countless therapists. I hired a nanny. But Crystal wanted nothing to do with us—except for my money, of course. That she continued to spend without compunction. In the meantime, I had a tiny infant to care for while overseeing a multimillion-dollar international telecommunications business. I also thought the best thing for Cadence would be to have her live at Carter Plantation with Aunt Elise, far away from all the paparazzi and where no one would have heard of Crystal Carter."

"When did you decide to divorce her?"

"I didn't. Can you believe it? Loyal to the end. Or stupid.

Anyway, she initiated the divorce. Her latest boyfriend actually wants to marry her. In all likelihood, he's as blinded to her issues as I was. She notified me through my lawyer this past October. Remember those heated meetings I was having with Calvin at the time?"

"Why didn't you tell me about her? Why wouldn't anyone talk about it?"

"I asked them not to. First of all, I don't want my staff to gossip about me if I can help it. And I suspected our former nanny—Caroline—may have left because of my mad wife. I didn't want you scared off. And after I met you, I especially didn't want to lose you. The first day I saw you running down the plantation road, you had a look of such joy, such innocent sweetness on your face. I was instantly captivated by you."

"How could you tell that? You were driving by so fast."

He smiled. "Why do you think I wrecked the car? I couldn't take my eyes off you. And then you pulled me out of my car. You rescued me. I had a presentiment then that you would be my savior. And you are so good with Cadence. I would watch you with her—your patience, your care, your love for her. I watched you and saw the mother Crystal would never be. And the wife. The more time I spent with you, talking, sharing, the more I sensed I had found a true soul mate, a kindred spirit, someone I could spend my life with and truly become one with. I began to consider Crystal's desire for a divorce as a good thing. In her quest to be liberated, she was, in fact, liberating me."

I couldn't bear to hear this rehearsal of his love for me. It was too painful a reminder of what we almost had.

"But now she doesn't want the divorce," I recollected for him.

"Now she's decided to sue for custody. I think she realized how little money she would have to settle for unless she had the baby as a bargaining chip."

"Maybe she's had a change of heart."

"Maybe. I doubt it. Unless . . ."

"Unless?"

"It's strange, but I think she may have been influenced by the part she's playing in *The Woman in White*."

"What do you mean?"

"Have you seen the show?"

"No, but I've read the book."

"There are some differences in the stories. But Crystal plays the part of Anne Catherick."

I gasped. "Then she really is the Woman in White!"

"Yes. And in the play version at least, her character Anne is impregnated by Sir Percival Glyde. He takes her baby away from her and drowns it. It's all quite terrible and is the horrible secret she's carrying. Anyway, I think it's possible, playing that part night after night, the idea of the baby became some sort of obsession in Crystal's unstable mind. It could be why she began harassing you with emails and phone calls and why she haunted Keswick Hall the night of the candlelight tour and followed you up the stairs to the nursery."

"But why would she set your office on fire or put the knife in your tire?"

"Well, now, remember she's either mad or she's acting a part, and there's a method in her madness. If she's delusional, she could be equating me now with the villain Sir Percival Glyde, thinking I took the baby from her. You'll remember he also shuts Anne up in a madhouse, and in the novel, he meets his doom in a fire. Or it could be she realized how little money she was entitled to and this is all simply a perverse plan to destroy me before we are divorced so that she could gain the baby and my wealth. I don't know what goes on in that brain of hers. All I know is that she is dangerous, and I'm taking out a restraining order on her and keeping Cadence and you as far away from her as possible."

"You needn't worry about me. I'll be leaving."

"Leave? You mean London? That's easy enough. The police already took your statement, and we can get you on a plane for home tomorrow. I'm so sorry we can't hold the wedding yet, but we can still take the cruise. I don't see any reason to cancel our trip."

"What about the fact that we won't be married?"

"That doesn't matter. Plenty of unmarried couples travel together these days. People do it all the time."

"That doesn't make it right. And I'm not one of those people."

Scowling, he studied me. "Jillian, we will still get married. It will just be a few months down the line, once we get everything settled. Since we intend to be married, why shouldn't we go ahead and take the cruise as planned?"

"Remember what you promised your aunt Elise? About not sleeping with me until we are married? I thought you meant that."

"Why, I did. But I thought we'd be married very soon."

"Ethan, I made a decision a long time ago to give myself only to my husband."

"Okay, I understand and I respect that. I'm sorry to have suggested otherwise. I could change the travel arrangements so that we have separate cabins. Would that satisfy you?"

"No, I'm sorry. I can't go on a cruise with a married man— even if we stayed in separate cabins. Ethan, I don't see any other recourse right now—I have to leave. We can't be married, so it's best for us both if I just go."

He mastered his annoyance. "All right. I have already made the arrangements for your return trip. I'll have a private taxi drive you out to Heathrow tomorrow morning. I'll be home as soon as I can get things squared away. Then we can figure out when to reschedule the wedding and the cruise."

"Ethan," I said quietly but doggedly. "I think I should really go—away from Carter Plantation and away from you. I don't think it's possible for me to live in the same house as you and see you daily when we cannot be married."

"Why not? I can promise to behave myself. I've been on good behavior, haven't I, and treated you with respect? We can go on as we have for the past few months. Calvin thinks all this will likely be resolved by the end of the summer. We can plan a September wedding. Virginia is lovely in September."

"Ethan, I for one do not believe I could simply go on as before. I cannot continue to treat you just as my employer. Not now. And any other relationship would be inappropriate. I can't do it. No, I simply will have to leave."

"You can't be serious! You can't leave me. You said so yourself the night I proposed to you. And what about Cadence? How can you abandon her?"

I saw a flash of fire in his eyes, but I resolved to withstand his anger. Up until this point I had not shed one tear, although they had been pent up for some time. I allowed myself to cry now. The release of emotion had its cathartic benefit for me as well as for Ethan. His anger quickly dissipated into dismay.

He gathered me in his arms, stroking my hair and kissing the tears from my cheeks. Oh, how I longed for his sweet kisses! Oh, how hard it was to resist him! I must, I had to leave him, or I would lose myself—and all that I believed to be right—to his will.

"Don't cry, my darling," he murmured. "We will work this out somehow. Just tell me you still love me."

"I do love you, Ethan!" I sobbed. "I love you too much. But I shouldn't, and you will not hear me say it again."

"Why not? I tell you, everything is going to be all right. I promise. We'll be married before autumn."

I could no longer argue with him, and so I simply wept. I knew what I had to do. Despite my love for him and for Cadence, I had to follow my conscience over my desires.

I determined that when I left Ethan Remington the next morning, it would be for good.

19

Ethan was up at dawn to see me safely off to Heathrow Airport. When the taxi pulled up, he embraced me tightly.

"Please think over everything I've told you," he pleaded in hushed tones. "Don't make a rash decision. Think of how I need you. Think of Cadence. Please. I'll be flying home in two days. We can talk things over then and agree on a course of action."

He kissed me then—a kiss fraught with desperate longing. A kiss of stolen sweetness mingled with sorrow. For me, a kiss of farewell.

"I love you, Jillian," he said as he helped me into the waiting taxi. "I'll love you forever. Think of me. I know we can work this out." One more soft kiss on my cheek and the door shut.

"Good-bye, Ethan," I said, raising my hand in a resigned

wave. I leaned my head back against the seat and whispered, "Good-bye, my love."

⊷✦⊷

I did think of him on the flight back to the States. I could think of little else. I rehearsed all the days and evenings I had spent in Ethan's company. I thought of darling Cadence and kind Elise Carter and my wonderful life at Carter Plantation. I considered all Ethan had shared. I reviewed all of the events in the last few months with the revelation of who CC was and what her possible motives had been. If Crystal's behavior had been as bizarre as Ethan had described—and after what I had personally experienced, I had no reason to doubt him—then surely she had broken the bonds of marriage, and there should be no impediment to Ethan's divorce.

But he was not yet divorced. He was a married man— even if his wife were at best mentally unstable and at worst murderously unhinged. He was still married and therefore not able to marry me. And even if he were divorced, could he remarry? Should he? Or should he hope for Crystal to come to her senses and wait for however long that might be? I knew that my foster family's church not only condemned divorce but held that remarriage for divorcees was not an option. But now I personally knew someone in an untenable marriage—a marriage in name only. Shouldn't there be mercy for one who had been abandoned, abused, or betrayed by adultery? Should someone so terribly wronged have to spend the rest of their lives alone because of the selfish sin of another?

My history lessons had taught me that churches had split over the issue of divorce and remarriage, going all the way back to Henry VIII. If kings and clergymen couldn't agree on this issue, how should I know what to do? It was all too much for me!

If God were heeding my prayers for wisdom, I must have felt his prompting to flee the temptation to stay with Ethan; and yet, why was this course of action like death to me? Hadn't I suffered enough—my hope and joy dashed? Was it really necessary for me to tear myself away from him whom I loved most?

But perhaps that was the point, after all. I knew only too well that I had put my love for Ethan above my love for God.

I also knew my own conscience would not allow me to be in a relationship with Ethan Remington while he was still married to Crystal Carter. Moreover, it now would be impossible for us to live under the same roof.

All this I considered and reconsidered on the flight back to Dulles Airport, where I was met by Jack driving the Cadillac Escalade, my former "nanny mobile." He and Marta warmly welcomed me home—how it hurt to hear those words!—as did Elise Carter. When I walked into the nursery, Cadence rushed into my arms and I hugged her tightly, reluctant to let her go. Tears coursed unchecked down my cheeks.

"Are you all right?" asked Sheryl, the temporary nanny.

"I missed her so," I said, feeling foolish as I put Cadence down and dabbed my face with a tissue.

"I don't blame you," she said. "She is so sweet, isn't she?"

"How did it go?" I asked.

"Good! She was a little clingy after you left and cried some the first night, but after that, she was a little trooper. Weren't you, pumpkin?" Sheryl scooped Cadence up and kissed her.

I liked Sheryl. She had a responsible head on her shoulders and a genuine love for children. As reluctant as I was to leave Cadence, I believed Sheryl would be a good nanny for her.

"Have you enjoyed working here, Sheryl?"

"I love it! I'm trying not to get too attached, because I know it's just a temporary job. But it's hard not to envy you. Still, if you decide that being married to Mr. Remington keeps you too busy, I would be happy to help out whenever you need someone."

"Would you like to make it a permanent position if you could?"

"Are you kidding me? I'd love to."

"Good. Then I'll recommend that to Mrs. Carter."

"I guess you'll be busy with the wedding and all and need an extra hand to help with the baby."

"No, actually. The wedding has been cancelled."

Sheryl's green eyes grew wide. "Oh my gosh! I'm so sorry!"

"Thank you. Things just didn't work out the way we had

hoped. So, I've decided it would be best to move on. I'll be packing up my things and will be out tomorrow morning."

"Oh no. I feel terrible for you."

"It's all right. It's my decision. Listen, I should talk things over with Mrs. Carter. But after dinner, would you mind if I look after Cadence and put her to bed? You can take charge again in the morning."

"No problem." She touched my arm empathetically. "I'm so sorry. It must be really hard for you to leave her."

"Yes, it is." I mustered a smile. "But it will be easier knowing that I'm leaving her in good hands."

"Don't worry. I will take really good care of her."

"I'm sure you will. Thank you."

I found Elise Carter sitting in the family room, engrossed in a novel. I broke the news to her as delicately as I could. I thought perhaps because of her adverse reaction to the news of our engagement, she might be relieved the wedding had been called off, but such was not the case. She seemed sincerely distressed.

"This is dreadful!" she cried. "I'm so sorry for you both. Poor Ethan! He's had so much disappointment already. I hate seeing him suffer any more. That Crystal! She does not deserve to bear the name of Carter! She's a disgrace to the family. Poor Ethan!" she repeated. "And poor you! Are you really leaving? Are you sure you have to? Oh, I suppose it would be best. It would be hard to keep things proper while living under one roof. But then Cadence—"

"I've spoken to Sheryl, and I think she'd love to stay on as Cadence's full-time nanny. I've watched them and believe she does a great job. Don't you agree?"

"Yes, yes, she does. So you think she'll stay? That's a relief. But do you really have to go?"

"Yes. I think it's best."

"But when?"

"Tomorrow morning."

"Tomorrow?" She looked up sharply, her white curls trembling. "So soon? Ethan isn't even back yet."

"I know. I think it will be easier to leave without him here."

"Does he know you are going?"

"Not exactly. I told him I didn't see any other option, but he asked me to reconsider. On the plane, I mulled it over and over, and I still believe it would be best for me to go."

"Oh, Jillian! This is terrible!"

"Yes," I agreed miserably. "It is."

"I'm so sorry. For Ethan, for Cadence, for you, for me. I'm sorry I wasn't more enthusiastic about your marriage, Jillian, when you first told me. You know, I was worried something like this might happen, and I didn't want to see you or Ethan hurt."

She took my hands in hers. "You are a dear girl, and I've come to think of you as one of the family. I will miss you. We all will miss you."

This was too much. I hadn't bargained on Elise Carter moving me to tears, but she had.

I squeezed her hands. "Thank you," I managed to choke out. "You are my family now, and I will miss you terribly."

She sighed and patted my hand. "There, there, my dear. You'll have to visit often. Perhaps in a few months' time, all of these impediments will be swept away and you and Ethan can be married after all. I'll write to you too, and keep you posted on everything that's happening. Where are you going? Where shall I write?"

"I'm not sure. And I don't want Ethan to know anyway because he would come after me. I don't think I could resist him. It would be best to stay away from him."

"But where should we send your paycheck?"

"I have direct deposit, remember? So that's not a problem."

"Please, Jillian. Leave me an address where I can contact you."

"I guess you could write to me in care of my foster family the Brookes. It's the same address you had for me when I first came here to work. But you must tell Ethan that I will not be staying there so there is no point trying to come after me or find me."

"Oh, dear." Her curls trembled again. "He is not going to be happy about that. In fact, he'll probably be furious with me. Jillian, you know Ethan will hire a private detective to find you. You won't be able to hide from him for very long."

"I know." I handed her an envelope. "Please give him this letter for me. I've told him that I don't want to be found unless circumstances change. That if he really loves me, he will respect my decision. He should let me go and not try to find me."

She sighed heavily. "All right, I'll do as you say. At least I'll know where to get in touch with you if I need to."

"Yes, you can leave messages for me at the Brookes, and they will let you know that I'm okay too."

"All right. I do hope all this gets sorted out quickly. What a nightmare!"

I couldn't have agreed more. We discussed other logistics, and then I excused myself to spend my final evening with Cadence.

That night I could not bear to part from her. I brought her into my bed, snuggling with her while she slept spooned against my side.

I don't believe I slept at all.

Just as the light of dawn crept into the nursery, I kissed her curly head one last time, gently laid her in her crib, and stole away from all I held dear.

20

As I drove my little Honda Civic away from Carter Plantation, I considered how different my feelings were from the day I had first arrived. Then, I was filled with anticipation and a lack of confidence. I had been intimidated by the size and grandeur of the estate. Now, I was filled with sorrow and a lack of purpose. I was overwhelmed with the sense of loss of family and of home.

The sky, overcast with thick gray clouds, reflected my mood. But the gray was not oppressively dark or threatening. It was a polite gray. By shading the sun's glare, it made my drive easier as I headed south over the rolling hills of Route 29.

I had no particular plan in mind but to escape before Ethan returned from England. The only friends I felt I could rely on were my foster family, the Brookes, and yet I knew I could not stay with them because that would be the first place Ethan would search for me.

But he would not know to look for me at the home of the younger Brookes. As far as I knew, he was unaware that Sharon, Diane, and their older brother, John, rented a house together in the countryside near the university town of Charlottesville. Although I had not attempted to contact them via phone or email in case he tried to trace me, I knew they would offer me a place to stay until I could map a new course for my life. And that's where I decided to go.

The older Brooke siblings shared a quaint yellow bungalow with white trim, circa 1920s, set on several acres of rolling hills in Albemarle County. Sharon, at twenty-one, the closest to me in age, was a third-year student in special education at the University of Virginia. Diane, twenty-three, had foregone a college education and worked as a church secretary. John, the oldest at twenty-six, had completed his masters in divinity from Princeton and now served as an assistant pastor in the same church as Diane.

Hoping someone would be home, I stood on the broad porch of the bungalow and knocked on the front door. I hadn't realized how exhausted I was until that moment. Not only had I not slept well in days, but I had not yet recovered from jet lag and the trauma of the recent events. Since I had stolen away from Carter Plantation before anyone else had awakened, I had neglected to eat any breakfast. Famished and fatigued, I nearly collapsed in Sharon's arms when she answered the door.

"Jillian? What are you doing here? For goodness' sake, what's happened?" She grasped my arms. "Are you all right?"

"May I come in? Could I possibly stay with you for a few days?"

"Of course! Come in." She held the door open for me. "Did you bring a suitcase?"

"I have my stuff in my car. I'll get it later. Listen, Sharon, I'm sorry to barge in on y'all like this without any warning."

"Don't be silly. We're your family," she said as she led me back to the kitchen. "You know you're always welcome with us. Can I get you anything to eat?"

"Sure, thanks." I sank into the nearest chair. "Anything will do."

"Breakfast or lunch?"

"Do you have some soup?"

"How about cream of potato soup and a grilled ham and cheese sandwich?"

I nodded. "Sounds perfect. But, Sharon, you don't need to wait on me. I can make it myself."

She frowned. "Jillian, I don't know what's going on, but you don't look like you are fit to do anything right now. You just sit there and I'll have this ready in a jiffy."

I complied, and she had a delicious lunch before me in

minutes. When I had nibbled half of the sandwich, she asked, "You look a little better now. So, what's up? Why the sudden visit? Don't you have a wedding to get ready for?"

I managed to choke out, "The wedding is off."

"What? You're kidding!"

I shook my head. "No, I'm not. I wish I were. Listen, I'll explain everything, but I would really like to lie down for a while first. I am so tired. After I've had a nap, I'll give you the whole story."

"Jillian, I'm so sorry."

"Yeah, me too. But it's for the best." I finished my sandwich and stood to carry my dishes to the sink. "Thanks for the lunch. That was super."

"I'll take those," Sharon said, whisking them out of my hand. "You go on upstairs. You can stay in my room. I have a spare bed. Remember, it's the blue one to the right of the stairs. I have to go to class, so you are welcome to sleep all afternoon if you like. Diane and John won't be home until around 5:30."

"Okay. I'll just take a little nap," I said as I trudged up the stairs. "Thanks so much, Sharon. You don't know how much I appreciate this."

⚜

I can't even remember lying down. I had a vague sense that while I was sleeping, Sharon and Diane, whispering to each other, came into the room several times. I could not rouse myself to greet them, but slept on. When I finally opened my eyes and stared at the clock, it read ten o'clock. I was disoriented by the time. I pushed myself upright and looked about. Sunlight was shining brightly into the snug bedroom.

"Hello there," Sharon said, reclining against her bed rest and surrounded by open books. "Welcome back to the land of the living! You've had quite a long nap now, and to tell the truth, Di and I were just a little bit worried."

"Is that clock right?" I asked, yawning. "Is it really ten in the morning?"

"Yep, it's Saturday morning. You slept straight through the afternoon and night—about twenty hours. I'd say you were one tired puppy."

"I can't believe it! I don't think I've ever slept that long in my entire life! Thank you for pampering me. I must have been really wiped out."

"I'll say. Do you want to take a shower?"

"Yes, thanks. I don't think I've gone such a long time without a shower either." I rose from the bed and smoothed out its sheets and comforter.

"I put some spare towels and a washcloth in the bathroom for you. They're the light blue ones. John brought in your suitcase and some of your things last night." She gestured to the other side of the room, where my belongings were neatly stacked. "Why don't you freshen up while I make you some breakfast."

"Sounds good. Thanks, Sharon." I knew she and Diane would be dying with curiosity about my change in circumstances. I appreciated her tact and consideration in waiting for me to have a chance to wash up and eat before they attempted to learn the facts and allay their concerns.

I enjoyed a luxuriously long, hot shower and changed into a pair of jeans and a T-shirt, pulling my hair back into a ponytail. I slipped on some flip-flops, which slapped the soles of my feet as I went downstairs, following the tantalizing aroma of frying sausage coming from the country kitchen.

The Brooke siblings had finished their breakfast long before, but Sharon had made some French toast and sausage for me. Again, I appreciated her consideration: although French toast was my favorite breakfast, she knew that I seldom took the time or trouble to make it for myself.

"Hmm, something smells fantastic!" I said as I entered the kitchen.

"Jillian!" Diane cried, springing from her chair to give me a big hug. "We're so glad you're here, aren't we, John?"

John Brooke rose and patted my shoulder. "Yes, welcome, Jillian. Here, have a seat." He pulled out an empty chair for me. "Sharon has made you breakfast."

"Your favorite." Sharon placed before me a plate piled high with French toast, artfully arranged with sliced strawberries and confectioner's sugar.

"Wow. This looks fabulous. Thanks so much."

I silently ate my breakfast. The girls chatted quietly among themselves as they cleaned up the kitchen, and John sipped a cup of coffee as he read the newspaper.

"Thank you. That was delicious," I said when I had finished and Diane had cleared my place. "Now, I know you all are wondering what I'm doing here, and I appreciate your patience. Sharon, did you tell them anything?"

"Just that you had said your wedding had been cancelled. That's all I know, except that you arrived yesterday afternoon looking like a refugee, and after eating some lunch, promptly fell asleep until this morning."

"Yes, the wedding is off. I don't know how to explain things except to just give it to you straight. To make a long story short, Ethan and I are not able to get married because he is already married."

"He's a bigamist?" gasped Diane.

"Well, no, because he didn't marry me. His wife had filed for divorce and he went to what he thought was the final hearing to sign the papers when she suddenly changed her mind. She refused to sign and demanded custody of Cadence."

"Who's Cadence?" John asked.

"The child I've been a nanny for. Ethan's baby. Apparently, her mother abandoned her when she was an infant. To be honest, I thought Ethan's wife was dead."

"So, let me get this straight," said John. "This Ethan guy deliberately misled you, promising to marry you when he knew he wasn't free to do so?"

"No. Like I said, he thought that the divorce would be finalized in time for our wedding."

"But you were led to believe that his wife was dead. So he never told you that she was alive?" John had taken on the adversarial tone of a prosecuting attorney.

"No. He didn't say she was dead either. I just misconstrued that from what people said."

"Your Ethan Remington sounds like an inconsiderate jerk," John pronounced.

"No, he's not at all!"

"Then he's a bad man. He shouldn't have led you on. He was probably trying to seduce you."

"That's not fair, John. You can't judge him like that. You don't know Ethan. You've never even met him. He just didn't ever want to talk about his wife. And I don't blame him. I've met her, and now I know why. She's a real whacko. She's really scary."

And I proceeded to tell them the entire story.

When I had finished, Sharon and Diane, who had been slack-jawed in amazement, stood to give me sympathetic hugs. John had sat quietly through the saga. He had listened intently, occasionally stopping me to ask a question to clarify a point.

"You poor thing!" The sisters fussed over me. "We're so sorry! What will you do now?"

Pressing his fingertips together, John spoke quietly. "Leave her alone, Shash, Di. The girl needs some time to think and pray, and we do too. Jillian, thank you for sharing. I'm sure that it was difficult for you to recount these events for us. Of course, you are welcome to stay here as long as necessary, but you need a fresh start, and at some point, for your own good, you should begin the search for a new job."

"That's what I intend to do," I said. "And I'd really appreciate being able to stay here in the meantime. I'll contribute to the household. I can help with chores, and I have some savings to defray my expenses. And if you learn of any job openings anywhere for a nanny or daycare provider, please let me know."

"All right. Let me give that some thought. The girls and I should probably talk this over and brainstorm some. And if it's okay with you, I'd like to share this with Mom and Dad to hear their opinion."

"That would be fine. But please—Ethan must not know where I am! He'll probably call your parents, so you'll need to warn them not to tell him that I'm here."

"Okay, I'll do that. Don't worry, they know how to keep confidences. I think I'll also talk to Pastor Bill at church. We may have an opening in our preschool program. That's not really my province, but I remember hearing that one of the teachers has had to take a leave of absence to take care of her elderly mother. If that spot is still open, would you be interested?"

"Of course!" I exclaimed. "That would be perfect."

"Good." John rose. "I need to prepare my Bible teaching for tomorrow, but we'll talk some more this evening after dinner. Jillian," he added gently, "I'm sorry this has happened.

You've been through a terrible shock, and I think you should continue to get some rest today."

"We'll make sure she takes it easy," Diane said, smiling.

"It's all settled then, Jillian." John extended his hand to me in a formal gesture. "Please consider this your new home."

21

While John worked on his Bible teaching, I spent the afternoon resting and reading as he had suggested. Sharon and Diane occupied themselves with their own reading and study: Sharon, with her college class work; Diane, with an online tutorial in desktop publishing. We sat together in the living room, sharing the comfortable silence of comrades working side by side in individual but common pursuits. John had arranged a study area in the adjoining dining room. Occasionally, I would look up from my novel and watch my friends, and a sense of peace and gratitude would sweep over me, for a time suppressing my despair.

The Brookes, bearing a decided family resemblance in their attractive features and penetratingly brilliant blue eyes, were all graced with remarkable beauty both inside and out. John and Sharon were tall, slender, and fair. Diane, petite like me, had thick dark hair that fell to her shoulders. Based on their physical attributes alone, any of the three siblings could have starred in one of Ethan Remington's films. In fact, on more than one occasion, John had been mistaken for Jude Law and asked for his autograph.

They had also been blessed with keen intelligence and multiple talents. Diane, with an artistic and organizational bent, loved to decorate and arrange the household. It fell to her to clean, shop, sew, and serve as the de facto housekeeper. Sharon, a natural nurturer, especially of children, enjoyed the cooking, gardening, and anything involving handicrafts, including the odd handyman job. John, not particularly inclined to domestic chores, nevertheless performed—without complaint—menial tasks such as taking out the trash and mowing the lawn. He also handled the finances of the household and served as the physical and spiritual guardian. As I gazed at them, each concentrating intensely on their studies, I considered that if I were to describe each as a bird, Diane would be a sweet brown dove; Sharon, a graceful white swan; and John, a vigilant tawny hawk.

I wondered how I would fit into their established routine and how I could contribute to their household. What personal gifts or talents could I bring to bless them? And what sort of bird was I? Perhaps a little sparrow: small and ordinary, but steadfast, diligent, and industrious. Yes, a sparrow would do. For God's eyes are on even the tiny sparrow.

I dozed off on the couch, and when I awoke I could smell

the aroma of chicken baking in a wine sauce emanating from the kitchen. When I wandered in, I was surprised to see that the table had been set for five.

"Who's coming for dinner?" I asked.

"Rebecca Olivier," answered Diane. "She goes to our church and she's a friend of Sharon's from the education school."

"And a very pretty one too," Sharon said with a sly smile. "We think she and John might like each other."

"Oh," I said, smiling back. "I see how it is."

The girls laughed and bantered back and forth as they resumed their preparations.

When Rebecca arrived, she was, indeed, quite pretty. In fact, with her long, shiny chestnut tresses and large doe-like hazel eyes, she was stunning.

John, certainly, must have considered her so. From the moment she came in, his usual assurance was found wanting. Stammering and blushing, he struggled—and failed—not to stare at her. I watched as his sisters exchanged knowing glances and smiles.

John had introduced me as their foster sister who had come to Charlottesville to find a new job.

"Really? What sort of work are you interested in, Jillian?" Rebecca asked with genuine concern.

"Well, I would like to work with children. I was a nanny for a toddler in my last job, but I like children of all ages." I added, "Although I do prefer preschoolers."

"You don't have a degree yet, do you?"

"No. I haven't been to college."

"I thought you looked too young to be a university graduate. But you do have a high school diploma, don't you? How old are you?"

"Twenty-one. And yes, I earned a diploma from the Brookes' home-school."

"The Brookes' Academy of Higher Learning," Sharon quipped with a laugh.

Rebecca lightly touched John's sleeve, and I watched the color rise in his cheeks.

"John," she said softly. "She could take Jackie's place in the preschool. We really need a teacher in the three-year-old class."

"Yes," he agreed. "I had mentioned that to her. I had planned to make inquiries on her behalf."

"I'll talk to my mom." Rebecca turned to me to explain. "She's the director of the preschool, and I can put in a good word for you if you'd like me to. Would you be interested in taking the three-year-old class?"

"I'd love to! That would be incredible!"

"It's not a big class or much of a challenge," John said. "You might grow quickly bored."

"I'm sure it's more challenging than taking care of one baby. But would your mom hire me when I don't have a degree?" I asked Rebecca.

"Why not?" she replied. "We're a private, church-affiliated school and can hire whomever we like. I'll talk to my mom tonight." She sat back in her chair, obviously pleased with the opportunity to help.

For my part, I was amazed. I had left Carter Plantation just the day before with little idea where I should go or what I should do. Now I sat at a dinner table with my foster family and a new friend. I had been welcomed into their home and offered the possibility of a good job.

It seemed, perhaps, that God's eye really was on this sparrow.

After a weekend of rest, I began my new life as a teacher at the preschool and daycare center of the Blue Ridge Community Christian Church, where Diane served as secretary and John as the assistant pastor. I loved teaching the three-year-old class. The children brimmed with ebullient curiosity and lavished on me their unreserved affection. For my part, I was soon devoted to each and every child and enjoyed implementing fresh ideas in the classroom. But despite the fulfillment I experienced in my new job, I found myself desperately missing Cadence. I hoped and prayed that she was too young to have developed as profound an attachment to me as I had to her. One of the greatest distresses over my broken engagement with Ethan was the necessity of abruptly leaving Cadence.

One afternoon when I had been working at the school for several weeks, I stayed a little later than usual to clean up the classroom and sort through and organize the learning and play centers. As I gazed over the bins of toys, I recalled how neatly and carefully Cadence's playroom had been set up—how thoughtfully and lovingly arranged. At this recollection, which led my thoughts inevitably back to Ethan Remington, I felt crushed with the weight of my loss and grief. Laying my head on my arms, I sat at a child-sized table and wept.

John found me in such a state. He was not unkind in his response. "Jillian?" he asked gently. "Are you all right? May I help you with anything?"

I looked up and wiped my eyes, embarrassed. "No, I'm fine. Sorry, just a momentary lapse."

"Are you unhappy with your position here?"

"No, not at all. I love the job. The children are adorable and the staff is amazing. Don't worry, I'm very happy here and very thankful that you and Rebecca were kind enough to recommend me."

At the mention of Rebecca's name, John blushed.

On my classroom bulletin board, I had mounted a montage of photographs I had taken of the children and school staff members. Included were several lovely pictures of Rebecca, who, now that the university spring term had concluded, was interning at the daycare center for the summer. The pictures caught John's attention, and his attention caught mine.

"Do you like the photos?" I asked.

He started. "Um—yes, they're very good. Impressive work."

"I mean, do you like the pictures of Rebecca?"

"Rebecca? Oh yeah. I hadn't really noticed. But, yes, they're very nice."

I smiled. "John, you can't fool me. I know you noticed hers."

Although I had lived with the Brookes for over five years, I had not had the opportunity to grow as close to John as I had to his sisters. He had often been away at college and then seminary, and yet the distance I felt between us had also been due to his reserved personality. I was naturally a shy person, but I felt that since the Brookes had regarded me as a part of their family, John should be to me like an older brother, just as Diane and Sharon were like sisters. Somehow, it did not seem right that there should be any formal constraints between us. I determined to speak frankly with him.

"Look, John, it's obvious you like Rebecca. Why don't you just ask her out?"

That caught him off his guard. "What do you mean? What makes you think I like her?"

"Oh, come on. Every time you're around her, you blush. Even if we just mention her name, you do. It couldn't be more obvious."

He blushed even more at my bluntness.

"And the first night I met her, when she came to dinner at the house, Diane and Sharon said you both liked each other. So, why haven't you asked her out yet?"

"Do you really think she likes me?"

"Of course, she does."

He pulled up a chair and sat down as one who seemed

quite relieved to talk about a subject that had been foremost in his thoughts, but as yet, unacknowledged. "Why do you think so?"

"She makes every excuse to drop by the house or the church. And she asks about you constantly. Yes, John, I'm sure that she likes you very much, and she's probably dying for you to ask her out."

He sat quietly for a few moments with a slight smile on his stern but handsome face. He seemed to savor this information, looking satisfied like a well-fed cat.

"I'd love to ask her out," he confessed. "But there's no point to it."

"Why not?"

"Because I don't believe in dating just for the fun of it. I believe you should only date someone you could envision marrying."

"And can't you envision marrying Rebecca?"

He shook his head. "No, I'm afraid not."

"But why not? She's beautiful, intelligent, sweet-natured, loves children, and has a strong faith. She will make someone a wonderful wife."

"Yes," he agreed. "She will. But not me."

"You don't think she'd make a good pastor's wife?"

"She probably would. But the trouble is that I don't believe she would make a good missionary's wife. And you may recall that after I complete this year of ministry at the church, I intend to go to Sierra Leone. I plan to leave, by the way, at the end of the summer."

"So soon?"

"Yes. My two-year commitment to the church will be up."

"Diane and Sharon can't be too happy at the prospect."

"No, but they understand I must follow the leading I have."

"But back to Rebecca. How do you know she wouldn't make a good missionary's wife? Perhaps she would seriously consider going to Sierra Leone with you."

"No. We've discussed it before. She definitely does not have a heart for Africa. She wants to pursue her education studies and be a teacher, right here in the United States. Besides, Sierra Leone is still quite unstable. It wouldn't be safe for someone like Rebecca."

"Then perhaps you should consider staying here," I argued. "What's wrong with continuing to be a pastor? Surely you've had plenty of opportunity to minister to the needy, right here in Charlottesville. And the university has grown more and more diverse. I've heard Pastor Bill say that God is bringing the nations to us. There are many foreign people right here who need to hear the gospel."

"That's true, and Rebecca has also argued that. But the bottom line is that I have a call from God to go to Africa. For a while, I had ambitions to be the pastor of a megachurch, but God spoke to me quite clearly that I should lay that desire down and prepare to be a missionary. Perhaps it is my cross to bear, but I cannot give up that call for Rebecca or anyone else."

"But what of her and her feelings? Her disappointments? Aren't you concerned for her?"

"Yes, of course, I am. But if I did give up my calling to be a missionary, I would be denying what I believe to be right, and I'm afraid I would grow to resent her. Besides, as you said, Rebecca will make someone a wonderful wife. I'm sure there are many young men—right here at the university—who are interested in her. Once she understands that I'm not the one for her, I'll bet she finds someone else in no time."

He rubbed his hands as if brushing them off. "But enough on that topic. You were crying when I came in. Since we are having an honest heart-to-heart talk, can you tell me what was making you so upset?"

"The truth is, I was really missing Cadence. I had grown to love her as my own child, and sometimes it just suddenly hits me how much I miss her."

He frowned. "Is it just Cadence you miss?"

"Oh, John," I sighed. "Of course, I miss Ethan too."

"I don't understand why you don't despise him after what he did to you."

"You of all people should know the importance of forgiveness."

"Forgiveness, yes. You can forgive but not forget. You shouldn't forget how he deceived you and how he was planning to marry you even though he already had a wife. The fact of the matter is that he was willing to turn you into an adulteress."

"John, I already explained that he thought the divorce would be finalized."

"I think the Scriptures are pretty clear. Even if he is divorced, he should not remarry, and if he does, he would be making an adulteress of you."

"But that is your opinion. You know as well as I that there are many different views on divorce and remarriage in the church."

"God hates divorce."

"Yes, he does. But divorce is not the unforgivable sin, is it? And anyway, the divorce was not Ethan's idea. Just the opposite! He did all he could to keep the marriage together, even though she had cheated on him and left him with a newborn. It was Crystal who wanted to divorce him. Is he doomed to a life of unhappiness and loneliness when he's already suffered terrible, not to mention life-threatening, rejection? How can you condemn Ethan when he was the one who was sinned against?"

"Because he had no business courting you while he was still married."

This discussion had taken an unsettling turn.

"Okay," I said. "I'm here, aren't I? I left Ethan. But I have to be honest. That doesn't mean it isn't still painful and that I don't miss him. I do. Just as I'm sure you will miss Rebecca and think of her with regret once you are over in Sierra Leone. And you shouldn't condemn Ethan. He didn't ask for any of this, and he did all he could to prevent it. You should pity him, not condemn him. Show some mercy, John."

"Fair enough. We'll leave it alone and agree to disagree." He stood. "With all this discussion, I never got around to telling you why I came by. I have a request to make of you."

"Sure. What is it?"

"You know I've been studying Krio to prepare for living in Sierra Leone. It would really help me if I had someone who would study with me—give me drills, review with me, that sort of thing. I was wondering if you'd be willing to do that."

"Wouldn't you rather have Diane or Sharon help you? They're more gifted in languages than I am."

"Sharon has her own studies to worry about, and Diane has no interest. Krio is a Creole language derived from English. You have a working knowledge of French and Latin and seem good with languages, so you could probably pick it up pretty quickly. I thought it might give you a challenge. Maybe it would help take your mind off other things. Would you consider it? It'd only be for the summer."

"Sure, John. I'd be glad to help you. I owe you everything."

"Good. Maybe we could start tomorrow?"

"How about tonight?"

"Perfect! That would be terrific." John smiled. "Thanks, Jillian, I really appreciate it. Tonight then."

22

*V*irginia summers are hot and humid, and this one was no exception. The early twentieth century bungalow I shared with the Brookes was not air-conditioned, but we managed to stay cool with enormous electric fans and gallons of iced tea. The house boasted a back porch as well as one on the front with an old-fashioned screened-in sleeping porch perched on top of the back one. We three girls moved our beds there for the summer and enjoyed sleeping in our own private tree house under the leafy protection of an old oak.

Thankfully, the church and preschool did have the modern amenity of air-conditioning. Diane and I spent the majority of our days working there in cool comfort while Sharon attended summer school classes at UVA, and John drove about the town of Charlottesville and the surrounding countryside, tending to the needs of parishioners. I helped with

Vacation Bible School and mothers' days out and served an occasional turn in the daycare nursery. Often I worked side by side with our capable director, Stacey Olivier, and her lovely daughter, Rebecca. I watched with interest as John's poignant prediction about Rebecca became a reality: she gradually gave up her hopes for John and began to entertain the attentions of an earnest law school student she met in the church's college- and career-age fellowship. John continued to blush profusely in her presence but did not register any surprise or regret when Rebecca and the future lawyer officially became a couple.

Sharon, Diane, and I joined the college- and career-age fellowship as well, and we held a home Bible study together, led by John, on Sunday evenings. I also returned to my old habit of attending church every Sunday, which I had neglected while I lived at Carter Plantation. My neglect had been gradual, eventually lapsing altogether. But in the Brooke household, where prayer and Bible reading were deemed as vital as eating and sleeping, I slowly recovered my former devotion. Over the course of that summer, my love for God at last toppled the idol I had made of Ethan Remington.

That is not to say that I ceased to love Ethan or to think of him often—especially in those moments when I was alone. But as often as I thought of him, I would strive to turn those thoughts into prayers; and I vowed never again to allow a person, no matter how precious to me, to take God's rightful place in my heart.

I did often wonder how Ethan and Cadence were faring,

if he had found any solace, or if he had made any progress in his custody and divorce settlement. Mr. and Mrs. Brooke had mentioned to John and the girls that Ethan had phoned them numerous times in an effort to learn some news of me. They had assured him that I was safe and well. Elise Carter had also called the Brookes weekly at first, but as the summer passed, her calls became less frequent.

The Brookes and I fell into a summer routine of spending several evenings a week after work in fellowship with our peers, and staying at home on the alternate nights. On our evenings at home, John enlisted my aid in the study of Krio, joined at least once a week by a Jamaican brother who, with his fluency in Jamaican patois, a Creole language closely akin to Sierra Leone Krio, helped both of us with the pronunciation and rhythm.

One evening late in August after we had worked very hard together to master a number of Krio proverbs, John asked if I would join him for a walk. A brief thunderstorm had swept away the close humidity, and the lingering light had faded to a soft glow. While crickets and katydids kept up their clamoring chorus, the evening sky, shot through with threads of purple and magenta, draped gently over the undulating hills and pasturelands to the blue mountains beyond.

"It's beautiful, isn't it?" I said quietly as we walked side by side.

"Yes," John agreed. Although he usually did not appear moved by such scenes of beauty, he added, "It's hard to find a much prettier view. Once I flew over the Midwest. It stretched absolutely flat as far as the eye could see. The farms were laid out in these perfect squares like a brown and yellow patchwork quilt. Then we flew over West Virginia and the landscape suddenly became greener and hillier. But when we flew into Virginia—I'll never forget it—it was so lush and green with these rich, rolling hills. Without a doubt, at least from the air, Virginia was the most beautiful state." He sighed. "I will really miss these views."

"Do you really have to go? Couldn't you stay here and be just as effective in serving the Lord?"

"Jillian," he said patiently, "we've been over this before. What surprises me is that more people don't heed the call to the mission field."

"I think it takes a very special person to heed that call."

"So do I." He settled on a large rock and gestured for me to join him. "You know, Jillian, I think you are such a person."

"Me?" I asked with astonishment.

"Yes, you. I've watched you over the last few months—how you've grown spiritually and emotionally, how you've taken on whatever task that's set before you without complaint, how you've ministered to all those little children day after day, and patiently and wisely dealt with their parents, and how you were willing to take up a foreign language you had no need of, simply to help me. You, Miss Jillian Dare, are quite a remarkable young lady."

"Why, thank you." I basked in his praise. I thought John

Brooke to be quite a remarkable young man. I admired and respected him deeply, although I found myself too often striving to please him.

"In fact, I don't know how I can possibly go to Africa without you," he added coolly.

A sudden chill sliced through me. "John, what do you mean? I can't go to Africa."

"I just listed all the reasons why you can and should."

"But I don't have a call to go! I'm just like Rebecca—I have never had the heart for it."

"You are not like Rebecca. You are a much stronger and steadfast person. You are also very gifted and bright. You are just the type of person we need on the mission field. I know you have your own dreams and ambitions that keep you from being content in a little preschool classroom. There's an orphanage in Freetown, attached to the mission there. They are desperately in need of a director. Think about it; think of how you could not only instruct a classroom of children, but you could have a major impact on the lives of hundreds of orphans who have been abandoned by civil war and AIDS."

He took my hand in his, but his touch held no warmth. "You, of all people, should know what that means to a child. Just think of the difference you could make!"

With this, he pricked my heart's core—ministering to an orphanage. Wasn't my entire life leading me to such a venture? But Africa? Did God really mean for me to spend my life in Africa?

"I will pray about it, John. Working for an orphanage does appeal to me. But I never really saw myself as a missionary to Africa. Give me some time to pray about it."

He smiled. "Of course. I know you will see the sense of it. But there's one more thing. I've been praying a lot for you and about this, and I believe God has even more specific plans in mind for us."

"What do you mean?"

"I mean that I believe God not only wants us to go to Sierra Leone, but he wants us to go together as a married couple."

"You've got to be kidding," I stated in flat disbelief.

He withdrew his hand. "No, I'm not. You know me better than that. I'm not one to kid around, especially about something this serious."

"You and I—married?"

"Yes. We get along well and we'd make a good team. Besides, it wouldn't be appropriate for us to travel together unless we are married."

"But John—you don't love me!"

"I do love you, Jillian, as a sister in the Lord."

"Exactly! But not as a wife! Not the way my husband should love me. You know you've never had those kinds of feelings for me. And I haven't for you. We are brother and sister, John. It's almost disturbing to think of you otherwise."

He drew himself up. "Excuse me?"

"You know what I mean. It would almost be like your marrying Sharon or Diane. It's ridiculous."

He stood up. "I think that's enough. Sharon and Diane are my natural sisters. You are not."

"But I could go to Africa as your sister. We can just tell everyone that I am."

"That wouldn't be true and they would know it."

"I am your foster sister, after all, and I'm your sister in Christ. A marriage just for appearance sake would be a sham."

"Jillian," he said in a quiet but authoritative tone, "my utmost desire is to do God's will. I believe he spoke to me that we should be married. It would not be a sham. I would be committed to you as a true husband, and I'm sure that with that commitment, loving feelings would follow. I would be true to you until death parted us."

"Actually, that could be fairly soon if I go to Africa. I could catch malaria or be captured by guerilla rebels."

"Now you're talking nonsense."

"Oh, really? You said Rebecca would not be the type to survive in Africa. She's much stronger than I am. I'm not sure you'd care a whole lot if I were to drop dead over there. You'd pray for me and move on with your plans."

"Okay, that's really not fair. This conversation is not going well, and we're saying some outrageous things we will regret later. We should go back to the house now." He began walking in that direction, and I meekly followed.

I felt ashamed for hurting him. I did long for his approval, and it would be the greatest honor to be the wife of a man like John Brooke. He was good, intelligent, and brave, and he loved God more than anyone and anything. And yet . . .

I scrambled to keep up with his long strides. "John?" I called. "John! Please slow down."

He did.

"I'm sorry. I said some pretty hurtful things. Will you forgive me?"

"There's nothing to forgive."

"Yes, there is, and I'm sorry. Look—" I laid my hand on his arm. "This idea was too sudden for me. I had no clue you were thinking this way. Would it be all right if we took a few days and prayed over it? You see, I need to know what God wants for me. Think about the Bereans. They examined the Scriptures for themselves to see if they were being properly taught, and God honored them for that. I need some time to seek the Lord for myself."

"All right, that's fair enough. But I will be leaving for the mission training school in Dallas in just two weeks. You could go with me as my fiancée for the training and then we could be married in December before leaving for Sierra Leone at the beginning of the year. You'll need to make a decision before I go to Dallas."

"Okay, I will. I will pray about it and think it over."

"Good. Good night, Jillian." At the door he leaned over awkwardly, brushing a kiss across my cheek.

The kiss could not even be called a holy kiss: it held no warmth and little love.

23

I cannot describe the level of tension that existed between John and me after his sudden proposal. He had declared he had forgiven me for my rash comments, but it became abundantly clear that he would not forget them. For many people a "defining the relationship" talk liberates them to express their love for one another. For us, it had the reverse effect. Our formerly congenial relationship was now uncomfortably awkward.

We continued as before with our studies of Krio, but with a strained reservation on both our parts. I now understood his ulterior motive for teaching me the language, and that awareness quickly turned the challenge into a chore.

Throughout that period of prayer and reflection, I constantly cried out to God for wisdom and guidance. John was gentleman enough not to allude to the subject again.

He trusted that I would be true to my commitment to seek God's will, which I did most earnestly. However, I was certain that he believed, without a doubt, what God's will would be. Despite my hurtful comments, John had set his heart on marrying me and taking me with him to Africa. To him, it was merely a matter of time until I would submit myself to that will.

But for my part, I could not. I desired God's will above all else, but at no time had I heard that still small voice calling me to Africa. And yet, John could persuade me to go as a fellow missionary. I would have been willing to make the sacrifices necessary to serve in the orphanage of which he had spoken.

But as his wife? To fulfill a mere functionary role? What frightened me most was the thought that over time I could grow to love John as a husband. He was handsome and admirable. He would be a good leader and father. But he would never love me truly as a wife, and if my own love waxed while his remained dutiful, it could drive me to despair. I would either be loved completely and without reservation, or I would not be loved at all!

The irony of my situation had not escaped me. Here I was, humble little Jillian Dare, offered marriage proposals by two exceptionally capable and remarkable men. One for love, but without God's sanction; the other had purported to be God's will, but without love. Rather than live in a constant state of regret or disappointment, I concluded that it would be far better never to marry!

As the summer drew to an end and John began packing up his things, I knew I had to give him my answer.

And it would not be easy.

❦

He chose to broach the subject once again after our last Krio session, when Diane and Sharon were out for the evening. As he neatly stacked the books and papers, he asked almost casually, "So, Jillian, what have you decided? Are you ready now to put all this knowledge to use and join me as a missionary to Sierra Leone?"

I paused, uncertain how to express my thoughts and feelings. I reached out and touched his hand with my own. "John, I've thought and prayed and thought and prayed about this. First, let me say that I am willing to go to Africa, and I am honored you would consider marrying me."

He smiled with a hint of triumph. "I knew it! I knew you would come around!"

"Wait! I haven't finished. Although I am willing to go to Africa, I still have not sensed a calling from God to go. And even if I were to go, I think it would be disastrous for us to contemplate marriage."

He withdrew his hand. "Disastrous? How so?"

"Look, John, I don't want to say anything else to hurt you. The bottom line is that we do not love each other."

"But we can learn to. It's God's will."

"You know, it's not fair for you to keep pulling out the

'God's will' card. Mankind has perpetrated all manner of ill under the banner of 'God's will.' All I know is that he has not spoken to me."

"Maybe he has and you're not listening!"

"Maybe so. But the Bible says to 'seek and you shall find, ask and it shall be given to you.' I've been seeking and asking. And I've been trying to listen. So far, nothing has resonated in my heart about going to Africa or joining my life to yours. And I also have some unresolved issues that should be settled before I take such a drastic step."

He frowned. "You mean with Ethan Remington, don't you?"

"Yes," I admitted. "I do."

"How can you possibly contemplate a future with that man after how he treated you? And even if he were to prevail in a divorce settlement and be 'available' "—he made exaggerated quotation marks in the air—"how can it possibly be God's will for you to marry a divorced man?"

"Even if that man had been wronged?"

"He would still be divorced, and God hates divorce."

"You know, John, divorce is not the unforgivable sin. Just maybe, God would have us show mercy and compassion to our brothers and sisters who have suffered through broken marriages—even more so when it's no fault of their own."

He shook his head. "You need to forget him."

"I can't. Whenever I pray, he comes to mind, and I feel compelled to pray for him."

"Fine! Pray for him. But don't hold out any false hopes

that you will ever be reconciled to him." He sighed. "Listen, Jillian, clearly you have not reached a conclusion yet, so it would be unwise for me to force the issue and push you to come to the mission training center with me. I think the best course is for you to continue to pray about it and come when you're ready."

"Or not," I said softly.

He stiffened but conceded. "Or not."

"Okay, John. I will continue to pray."

He politely excused himself to go to his room just as Diane and Sharon returned home. They offered to help me clean up the kitchen.

While we washed and stacked the dishes, Sharon asked, "So, what's going on between you and John?"

"What do you mean?" I cautiously returned her question with another one.

"Did you argue about something? Things have changed between you two. It's like there's some sort of unresolved tension."

"He didn't tell you that he wanted to court you, did he?" Diane ventured.

"No. The truth is he skipped that part and just came out and asked me to marry him."

"Marry him?" repeated Diane with breathless incredulity.

"What?" Sharon asked in a more exasperated tone.

"That's right, he asked me to marry him. Actually, it was more like him telling me we should get married."

"Just like that, with no courtship or dating?" Sharon nearly sputtered. "But, but—have we missed something?"

"No, you haven't missed a thing!"

"I'm sorry to sound so surprised," said Diane. "I shouldn't be. I have noticed that he's taken a real interest in you. He asks about you a lot and keeps tabs on how things are going at the preschool and all. It's just that he's never shown anything but brother-sister type feelings for you. If you know what I mean."

"Exactly! He hasn't."

"But I'm sure he must if he's contemplating marriage. Oh, Jillian," Sharon cried. "It would be perfect if you and John were to get married! Then we'd be sisters for real, and he'd stay right here and give up his plan to be a missionary to Africa."

"No, he won't. He still intends to go to Sierra Leone. It's just that he wants me to go with him, and he believes that we'd need to be married."

The girls grew extremely quiet while that information registered.

"Do you mean," Diane finally said, "that he thinks that you should go to Sierra Leone with him and that's the only reason he has proposed to you?"

"Exactly!"

"Oh no!" Sharon groaned. "What can he be thinking?"

"Not much," Diane said dryly. "You didn't agree to this, did you?"

"No. I told him that I'd be willing to go to Africa and work in the orphanage in Freetown, but I have not had a call from God to do so. And I could not marry him, simply because we do not love each other." I sank into a chair at the kitchen table and threw down my dish towel. "We had this discussion about two weeks ago. I promised to pray about it and I have, but I still have not sensed any call or confirmation in my spirit that this plan of his is God's will for me."

"But haven't you ever heard the four spiritual laws according to the Brookes?" asked Sharon with a thin smile.

"What?"

"You know: law number one is 'God loves you and John Brooke has a wonderful plan for your life,'" she quipped.

"Be serious, Sharon," chided Diane.

"I am. Sadly, I am. You know how he can get, Di. He thinks he's been to the mountain and that everyone else should follow him there. He can be so stubborn!"

"Well, so can I," I said. "I'm sure he thinks so, anyway. Since our first talk, things have been very strained between us. Tonight after we finished our Krio lesson, he brought it up again. He's leaving soon, you know, and wants me to go to Dallas with him—as his fiancée."

"This is crazy!" Sharon cried. "You're not going, are you? As much as I love you and would be thrilled to have you for a sister-in-law, I do not think you should go to Sierra Leone—unless of course, that is where God has called *you*."

"That's exactly what I told John again tonight. I promised to keep praying, and I will. But I need a clear sign. Something. I can't go just because John thinks it's a good idea."

"Nor should you," Diane said. "It's a very serious step. Things have settled down a lot over there, but it's still a volatile region and not particularly safe."

"Maybe that's why he wants us to be married—so we can stay together and he can keep me under his wing."

"Maybe. But that is not enough reason to pledge your lives together." Diane did a final cleaning sweep of the kitchen. "We're so sorry he's put you in such an awkward spot. We'll be praying for you that God will speak clearly to your heart."

"And that he'll straighten out John too!" added Sharon.

"Thanks, y'all. I really appreciate it."

"Are you coming up now?" Diane asked as she held her hand to the light switch.

"I'll be up in a few minutes. You go on. I'll get the light. I just need a little more time to think and pray."

"Okay, good night." Both girls gave me hugs before climbing the stairs.

I wandered out to the back porch. I sat on the steps and gazed up at the night sky. The stars hung low and luminous, sprinkling light across the heavens.

O God! My heart cried out. *Please show me what to do! Let your kingdom come and your will be done in my life. Give me a sign! Please speak to me!*

The stars winked. A dog barked in the distance. The crickets' chorus filled the heavy, humid night air.

Cutting through it all, the telephone rang shrilly.

I sprang to my feet and dashed into the kitchen, the screen

door banging against my heels. I picked up the phone, cutting short the ring.

"Hello?"

"Jillian, is that you?"

"Yes, who's this?"

"It's Mom Brooke. I'm so glad I caught you!"

"Is anything wrong?"

"I don't think so, but we had a call tonight from Mrs. Carter. She would really like to get in touch with you. Could you give her a call? I have her number if you need it."

"It's okay, I know it. Should I call her this late? Did she sound like something's wrong?"

"I just hung up with her so I think it would be fine. She sounded a little anxious. I really think it would put her mind at ease to hear from you as soon as possible."

"Okay, Mom. I'll give her a call. Thanks."

"Bye, honey."

"Bye." The connection clicked to silence. My heart beat rapidly. I held the phone in my hands for a few moments, drawing in deep draughts of air in an effort to calm myself. With a fortifying gulp, I punched in the numbers I knew so well.

It only rang twice and then I heard the warm, welcoming voice of Elise Carter saying, "Hello, this is Carter Plantation."

"Mrs. Carter? This is Jillian."

"Jillian! Oh, my dear girl, I am so glad to hear from you! It's so good to hear your voice."

"It's good to hear your voice too. Mrs. Brooke said you had called. Is everything all right?"

"Yes, everything's fine! I just have some really good news for you. Ethan called from England, and the divorce has been finalized. Isn't that marvelous? The custody case will be heard tomorrow, but he fully expects it to go our way too. He always asks if I've heard anything from you, so I just had to try to reach you. He will be flying back after the hearing. Would you consider coming home, Jillian? We'd all love to see you."

I could barely process all this information, but I clearly saw the course I should follow. I would never know for certain what I was to do with my life until I had resolved my relationship with Ethan Remington.

"I'd love to come—at least for a visit."

"That'd be wonderful! Ethan will be so glad!"

"But, Mrs. Carter, please don't say anything to Ethan. Let it be a surprise."

"Oh, all right!"

I couldn't help but smile at her delightful chiming laugh.

"I'll have to wrap some things up here in the morning before I can leave," I said. "But I should be there by suppertime if that's okay."

"That'd be perfect! I'll ask Marta to cook up a good old-fashioned Southern dinner. We'll kill the fatted calf!" She laughed again. "We'll have you all settled in to surprise Ethan on his return. Oh, honey, I'm so glad!"

"Me too!" I laughed with her and then said good-bye.

Thank you, God! I breathed as I hung up the phone.

I had not heard God's voice in my desperate pleading. I had not heard it through John's haranguing. I had not heard it in the silence of the stars or the singing of the crickets. But perhaps, just perhaps, there are times we can hear him speak through our circumstances.

I was about to find out.

24

Early the next morning, John Brooke had a men's breakfast to attend, and I stayed in my room quietly packing until I heard him leave the house. I knew that he would try to persuade me not to go, and I wanted to spare us both the painful feelings that would arise if we prolonged our discussion on the nature of our relationship. I would continue to pray about it, as I had promised to do, but I was convinced that God had opened a door for me to explore.

Now that Ethan was officially divorced, it might be possible for us to marry. I was aware that according to John Brooke's scriptural understanding of divorce and remarriage, Ethan should remain single or be reconciled to Crystal—unless she remarried, and reconciliation was then forever impossible. I struggled with this rigid interpretation, also held by others in our church, because it did not take into account the ongoing and very real circumstances of the divorce: adultery, abandonment, and even abuse.

I had wrestled with the entire passage on marriage in Paul's first letter to the Corinthians and had been struck by the words, "But if the unbeliever leaves, let him do so. A believing man or woman is not bound in such circumstances; God has called us to peace." Once Crystal decided to leave, didn't that mean Ethan was no longer bound? If she had taken up with another man—whether or not she legally married him—wouldn't that be sufficient evidence that reconciliation was not possible? Was it fair to condemn Ethan to a life of singleness and celibacy based on the actions of his former spouse? Was it fair for Cadence to have to grow up, abandoned by her mother, with no mother to take her place? Or, as I had expressed to John, shouldn't the church extend grace and mercy to those who unwittingly find themselves devastated by divorce?

The right course would certainly be clearer if Crystal remarried, but if she did not, and continued to live in an adulterous relationship, what then? What would I—in my own individual conscience—choose to do? I had concluded that I must make my own decisions before God. When my time came, I alone would stand before God and give account of my life and choices. Therefore, I would not allow anyone else to make those choices for me.

On the other hand, Ethan's ardor for me may have cooled since my departure and I might discover upon my return that he no longer wished to marry me. In such a scenario, all my internal debates would be to no avail. I believed I had reached a spiritual relationship with God strong enough to withstand such a disappointment. I knew I could not return Ethan to his idol status in my life. I also knew that even if he wanted me, I would not be content for him to make an idol of me. God must be preeminent in both our lives, or our marriage would fail as well.

All these thoughts roiled in my mind as I packed and arranged details for my absence. I had been due some vacation time before the school year began again and decided to use it now. After speaking to Stacey Olivier on the phone, we settled that Rebecca would cover my summer duties at the daycare center until Labor Day. As soon as I knew my course of action, I would notify them whether or not I would return to work for the fall term.

Sharon and Diane helped me carry my things out to my car.

"Okay," Sharon said. "You're not taking everything, so can we assume you won't be gone long?"

"I honestly don't know, Shash," I said as I closed the trunk door and heard it click in place. "I'm viewing this as a two-week vacation. I may stay at Carter Plantation for the entire time, or if things aren't working out, I may drive down to Harrisonburg and visit the family there. All I know is that last night I prayed and pleaded for some sort of sign, and then your mom called and connected me with Mrs. Carter. I believe I should go to Carter Plantation, at least for a visit. But I don't know where this will lead. I only know that if I don't go, I will never have any resolution."

"Don't worry. Di and I are completely behind you."

"But we're wondering," Diane added, "what should we tell John?"

"Yes, what shall we tell John?" I sighed. "I think you should tell him that I'm taking a little vacation. That I decided to visit some friends and take a personal retreat. I'll continue to pray about going to Sierra Leone and hope to resolve everything soon. All that is true. I don't think you need to tell him where I'm going. It will just upset him. I don't want to spoil your last few days with him before he leaves for the mission school."

"That seems fair enough," Diane said.

Both girls hugged and kissed me, wishing me well.

My drive to Fauquier County passed pleasantly. The views of the Virginia countryside always inspired me with delight, but the sky blazed white with heat and humidity on this typical August dog day. I was grateful for the air-conditioning in my car and looked forward to the cool comfort of Carter Plantation.

<hr />

I did find cool comfort, but was surprised and dismayed at the cool reception I received.

Jack, unsmiling, greeted me. "Hi, Jillian. I'll take your luggage. You'll be sleeping in the rose guest room, next to

Miss Elise's room. You should go to her. She's in the family room."

When I entered the kitchen, Marta nodded to me with a grim smile and quickly turned back to her work. Only Ranger, his tail wagging, rose from his bed by the hearth to give me a warm welcome.

"Jack," I asked as we passed through into the hallway, "is anything wrong?"

"Something's happened. We've had a terrible blow," Jack answered. He paused and set down the luggage. "I don't know how to soften this, so here it is: Ethan was in an accident."

"An accident?"

"Yes, a car accident."

"God have mercy!" Fear gripped my heart. I managed to whisper, "Is he dead?"

"No, but he's in critical condition. We're not sure of the full details, so it would be best for you to hear it straight from Miss Elise. I have to warn you—she's pretty much a wreck right now, so try to be strong for her sake."

I entered the family room where Elise Carter sat curled up like a small child in her favorite chair. It was clear she had been weeping. When she spied me, she burst into a fresh round of loud sobs, and held her arms out to me the way Cadence would.

I ran into her embrace and we held each other as we both wept. She could not speak, but sobbed in broken phrases, "Ethan . . . poor boy . . . almost lost him . . . terrible accident . . . that Crystal . . . why did he try to save her . . . poor Ethan!"

I pulled myself together first, but she continued to vent her fear and sorrow in heartrending, inarticulate sobs. The brash ringing of the phone interrupted us.

"You get it," Elise murmured. "I can't . . ."

I picked up the receiver.

"Hello?" My voice shook. "Carter Plantation, Jillian Dare speaking."

A rich baritone voice, which I hadn't heard in several months, came over the wires.

"Jillian? This is Calvin. What the blazes are you doing there?"

"I thought I'd be here for Ethan's homecoming. Calvin, what's happened?"

"I'll explain everything, but first tell Elise that Ethan has stabilized. He's not out of the woods yet, but he's stable enough that they are going ahead with the eye surgery now."

"Eye surgery?"

"Yes, glass flew into his eyes. They're not sure yet if he'll keep his sight."

"But—"

"Jillian, please tell Elise what I just told you."

"Okay, sure. I'm sorry." I repeated the information to Mrs. Carter, who nodded that she understood. "Now, Calvin," I said, turning back to the phone, "please tell me everything that happened. Mrs. Carter is very upset and hasn't been able to talk about it. How did this happen?"

"We had the final custody hearing this morning. Of

course, Ethan has a very fine barrister representing him, but I've been with him to give my legal advice and moral support as a friend. The case went completely our way. Ethan had chosen not to press charges against Crystal, but the evidence against her in terms of setting the fire at Keswick Hall made a pretty strong case against her genuine concern for the baby. Not to mention that she had abandoned her as a newborn and had never shown an interest in her until she realized she wouldn't be entitled to a large financial settlement—unless she could claim childcare costs."

"Calvin," I interrupted, "I want to hear about the case, but please, first tell me about the accident."

"I'm getting to that. The judge made his ruling in our favor. Ethan was granted full custody, and Crystal was left with nothing, not even visitation rights. Of course, we were ecstatic. When we came out of the courtroom, though, we ran into a swarm of paparazzi. Crystal was nearly engulfed by them. She looked really frightened and beside herself. I don't know where that supposed fiancé of hers was today, but Ethan saw her predicament and shoved through the reporters to rescue her, telling her that he would give her a lift wherever she wanted.

"He was driving the Aston Martin. She got in the front and I rode in the back. Ethan sped away from the paparazzi and headed down the Victoria Embankment. When it seemed like we had made a clean escape from them, he asked Crystal where she wanted to go. She didn't answer.

He asked again. Right before my eyes, she grabbed the steering wheel and pulled the car smack into the embankment wall. I swear to you, if ever I saw a demonic look on someone's face, I saw it on hers as she grabbed that wheel."

"Oh no! Oh my gosh, what happened then?" I asked. "Were you hurt?"

"I'm okay, thanks. Just some whiplash and a little shell shock. I was in the backseat, remember? But the car was totally crushed on the passenger side and in danger of going up in flames. I jumped out and tried to get Ethan out too. He wouldn't leave Crystal and was trying to pull her out. But she was already dead. You could see she was. She must have died on impact. But he still tried to save her. Then the car caught fire, and I had to haul him out of there. But not before his arm was burned."

"His arm?"

"Yes, he burned his left arm pretty badly—second- and third-degree burns. They worked on that this afternoon. He'll lose some range of motion but keep his arm, thank God. They'll be able to give him some skin grafts eventually. But he's in the ICU now."

"What else is wrong with him?"

"He's pretty cut up. They've been running all kinds of tests to make sure there aren't any internal injuries."

"Is he conscious?"

"Yes, but he's pretty doped up, so he's not really with it."

"And Crystal . . . you said she's . . . ?"

"Yes, she's dead." He sighed. "What a tragic waste of a life."

"I'm sorry," I breathed.

"Why should you be sorry for her?"

"It's all so sad. She was a tormented human being whom God loved. Ethan loved her too, once. And she was Cadence's mother. This must have been terribly traumatic for him. I'm so sorry."

"Why, you beat all, girl! No wonder Ethan is so besotted with you. He was devastated when you took off last May, by the way."

Those words emboldened me. "Calvin, which hospital is he in?"

"St. Thomas."

"Where is that?"

"Lambeth, right across the river from Westminster and the Houses of Parliament. Why?"

"I'm coming. If there is space available, I will get a flight out tonight."

"Wow, really? Well, okay. That would be super. But let me think. Um . . . I'll book a flight for you and call you back with the details."

"No, thank you, Calvin. I'll book it myself. I've been working all summer and have a good amount of savings. I can cover it—it's not a problem, really."

"All right. That's cool. Then let me give you a number where I can be reached."

He did so and told me that he would reserve a room in

the hotel where he was staying. We discussed a few more logistics, and he promised to call if he had any updates on Ethan's condition.

"One more thing," he added before saying good-bye. "Don't turn on the news. There's bound to be something on TV about the accident. I don't think it would be a good idea for Elise to see any photographs of the crash. You neither for that matter."

"Okay," I quickly agreed. "And, Calvin, in case I am delayed, please don't tell Ethan that I'm trying to come over. I'd like to surprise him, and I don't want him concerned about me or distracted from getting better."

"I can't talk to him right now anyway, so you have no worries there."

"Thank you for all you've done to take care of him."

"Sure thing. Hey, please keep him in your prayers. He's going into surgery soon."

"Yes, of course. He's always been in my prayers. Thanks for filling me in, Calvin. Take care, and hopefully I'll see you tomorrow."

We said our good-byes and then hung up. I turned to Elise.

"I'm sorry to desert you as soon as I walk in the door, but I'm going to try to find a flight to London tonight. May I use the computer to check the airlines? And would Jack be able to drive me to the airport?"

Elise jumped to attention. "Of course, of course. But do you think I should go too?"

I put my hand on her arm. "The best thing you can do is to stay here and look after Cadence. I'm sure Ethan will rest much easier knowing she's under your charge."

"Oh yes, the baby. And you haven't even had a chance to see her yet. Will you have time to?"

"I hope so. But let me go online first. I need to reserve a flight as soon as possible."

I did a quick search on some travel websites and found a seat on an outbound flight of United Airlines, leaving at nine o'clock that evening from Dulles. The remaining economy seat—inconveniently stuck in the back of the plane by the toilets—would yield a far different flight experience than flying first class with Ethan, but I was grateful to be able to book anything. I would have enough time to change into more suitable travel clothes, share a meal with Mrs. Carter, and spend some time with Cadence before having to leave for the airport with Jack.

I had worried that Cadence would forget me, but I needn't have. When I walked into the nursery, I found her playing on the floor with her new nanny.

Sheryl looked up in surprise. "Jillian! You're back!"

Cadence stared at me for a few moments. Suddenly her face lit up with recognition, and she ran to me, lifting her arms.

I swooped her up and held her tightly. "Hi, sweet girl. I missed you so much!" I lavished her with kisses until she squealed. "Hmm, hmm, hmm! I could kiss those chubby cheeks all gone. I love you *so* much!"

"Wuv you sooo much!" she echoed.

"I can't believe she's talking, and I've missed it all," I said as I put her down and joined her and Sheryl on the floor.

"She has a lot of words now," said Sheryl, "and can put together some simple sentences. She's quite a storyteller, actually. Well, not that I can really understand what she's babbling about, but it's really cute. So . . . ," she asked with some hesitation, "are you back for good?"

"I'm not sure. Did you hear about Mr. Remington's accident?"

"Yes. Isn't it awful?"

"Yes," I agreed.

"I feel so bad for Cadence! First her mother deserts her and then she kills herself. And now her dad is fighting for his life."

"Yes, I know. It's unimaginable."

"Have you heard any news on how he's doing?"

"Mr. Cole just called to say that he's stabilized and they're going ahead with the eye surgery. I decided to fly over, and I've booked a flight for tonight, so I'll be leaving again soon. I just wanted to spend a little time with Cadence while I'm here."

"Sure. Would you like me to stay or would you prefer to have some alone time?"

"Why don't you take off for a couple of hours? I'll have to leave here around six to give me enough time to get through security at Dulles. I can't miss this flight. Could you possibly take over again then?"

"No problem. That would be cool. I'll call Corinne and tell her she doesn't have to come by today." Standing to leave, Sheryl added, "I sure hope Mr. Remington will be all right."

"Yeah, me too. Anyway, thanks for sharing Cadence with me. It seems that she's thriving under your care."

"Thanks. She's a sweet baby and I've enjoyed taking care of her. I'll see you later." Sheryl quietly slipped out of the room.

Cadence began to pout when she heard the door shut, but I quickly distracted her.

"How about a story, sweet girl?" I asked.

She perked up right away and began lugging several large books over to me. I picked her up and snuggled with her while I read aloud. When it came time for her nap, I couldn't resist spoiling her with a bottle and singing to her while I rocked her to sleep. But she fussed and squirmed and tugged at my ponytail until I realized what she wanted. I let down my hair, and her little fingers twisted around one of the strands. She sighed with contentment.

It nearly broke my heart.

25

I remember little of the flight over to England except for it being arduous and interminable. After clearing immigration, I took the Heathrow Express into Paddington Station and a taxi from there to the small but posh hotel in Westminster where Calvin had secured a room for me. Pausing only long enough to change my clothes and brush my teeth, I caught another cab to St. Thomas, a sprawling hospital complex on the opposite side of the Thames. Karla and I had ridden past it on our London bus tour, never imagining at the time that Ethan would be a patient there one day. Everywhere I looked, the London tabloids buzzed with the shocking news of Crystal Carter's suicidal crash into the Victoria Embankment and Ethan Remington's struggle for his very life.

I found the hospital lobby overrun by reporters, but since

I appeared inconspicuously dressed in jeans and a sweater with my hair in a ponytail, no one gave me any notice. Fortunately, Calvin had left word at the reception desk that I was to be admitted as a visitor. I learned that Ethan had been transferred from the surgical recovery unit to a private room in the burn ward. My heart lurched along with the elevator, and I gripped the handrail to steady myself. When I emerged, I spied Calvin stretched out on a couch in a waiting room lounge.

"Calvin?" I spoke softly.

He scrambled to his feet. "Jillian! You made it!"

I was surprised and pleased when he embraced me.

"How's Ethan?"

"He's okay! The good news is he's out of the woods now and no longer in critical condition. The doctors haven't found any other internal injuries, and he came through the eye surgery just fine. The bad news is that they won't remove the bandages for a few days, and until they do, we won't know for certain if he lost any of his vision."

"Is he awake?"

"Yes, he's awake. He's been out of surgery for several hours now. But he was just transferred up here from recovery a little while ago, so I was giving them a chance to settle him in his room. He should be ready now, though. Why don't you go check?"

"Is he allowed to have visitors?"

"Yes, but the nurse said to keep the visits brief and he's supposed to keep very still. You go ahead. I'll just stay here and continue my little nap. I'm sure he's sick of seeing me anyway. He's in 316, down the hall, on the right."

"Thanks, Calvin."

I headed down the corridor, checking the room numbers, my heart thumping harder and faster with each step. The door to room 316 stood ajar. I could see Ethan lying prone in the bed. Bandages covered his eyes, pushing his thick, dark hair up off his forehead. His left arm was also heavily bandaged. Even though he looked like a war casualty, my heart rejoiced to see him. His head cocked to one side as he listened intently to a TV news program. He stirred when I touched the metal door.

"Is someone there? Nurse?" he called. "Would you bring me some water, please?"

I walked in, picked up the plastic pitcher, and poured some water into a drinking cup. My hand trembled so that water splashed out onto the tray. He was polite enough not to comment on my apparent clumsiness. I raised the head of his bed slightly and held the cup to his lips while he drank.

"Thank you," he said, sighing heavily. "That's good. Your perfume, by the way, Miss, smells heavenly. It reminds me of some I once gave to someone very dear to me. But you aren't the nurse I had earlier, are you? Has the shift changed already?"

"Your nurse was busy," I said as calmly as I could. "I heard you call and came in to assist you."

He was startled when he heard me speak. "You're American—your voice . . . you . . . who are you?" he demanded.

"Someone still very dear to you, I hope."

"Impossible!" he cried. "That perfume, your voice—you sound like . . . oh, but I can't see! Give me your hand!"

He flailed with his good hand until I caught it in my own.

He rubbed his large hand over my small one. "These little fingers feel like my Jillian's," he said hoarsely. "Can it be you? Jillian? Is it really you?"

"Yes, I'm Jillian! It's really me."

"No, no. You can't be real! It's the drugs. I—I think you must be some sort of hallucination. You don't know how many times I've dreamt you would come. I must be dreaming now. I'll wake up soon and you will be gone. And then I shall be all alone again." He pressed his lips against the palm of my hand.

"You're not dreaming, Ethan. I'm really here. You can smell my perfume—the perfume you gave me when we were engaged—you can hear my voice, and now you're kissing my hand."

"My dear girl!" he cried. "Come closer." Encircling my waist with his right arm, he drew me toward him and held me tightly. "You are small like my Jillian."

"I am. I am the same size and have the same voice, and I still have the same heart." I lightly lay my head against his chest. "I'm here, Ethan."

"My dear, darling girl!" he said, stifling a sob and hugging me even tighter. "You came back to me. I can't believe it. You came back!"

"Yes. And I shall stay as long as you need me."

He hesitated before replying, and in that hesitation I wondered if I had overstepped myself.

"And how will you stay?" he asked testily. "As Cadence's nanny? As my nurse?"

I answered with caution. "However you wish."

"You are too young to be stuck with nursing a broken-down man like me." He groaned. "How can you bear even to look at me? I must be ghastly. Tell me the truth. Do I repulse you?"

I understood then why he had hesitated. "No, Ethan, for goodness' sake! You could never repulse me. You've never looked better to me."

"But when the bandages are removed, you may decide differently."

I tried to lighten the tenor of the conversation. "To be honest, your hair is a mess. Where's a comb? Let me comb out that mop of yours."

I found one on his bed table and gently untangled his hair.

"Hold still!" I chided him. "You're not supposed to be moving about. Honestly, you squirm more than Cadence. There," I said as I put back the comb, "now you're much more presentable."

I lay my head back on his chest. "The truth is, Ethan, I don't care how you look. I am just thankful you're alive!"

"I wish I could see you," he said, drawing me closer. "But to hold you again—it is enough. It is enough."

The nurse knocked lightly on the door.

"Oh!" I exclaimed, righting myself. "I'd better go. Calvin told me to keep the visit brief."

"Wait!" Ethan held me back. "Please kiss me before you go. I must have one kiss to remember—in case I do wake up and discover that you were merely a dream."

"Don't worry. I will do my best to be here when you awaken. But here's your kiss." I kissed him gently on his lips. "And here and here." I kissed the bandage over each of his eyes. "And here." I kissed his forehead. "And here." I kissed his bandaged arm.

"My arm was badly burned," he said. "They'll be putting me in a whirlpool bath to remove the charred skin. It's pretty ghastly. I may need skin grafts."

"Yes, I know. Calvin told me. You were very brave. It just makes me love you all the more."

"She's dead. Crystal—she died in the accident. She grabbed the wheel. There was nothing I could do. I tried to stop her—I tried to save her—it was horrible!"

"It wasn't your fault, Ethan," I soothed. "I'm so sorry that it happened. But you must believe that it wasn't your fault. You did all you could for her."

"Excuse me," said the nurse, knocking again as she breezed into the room. "Sorry, Miss, but you'll have to leave. The doctor wants to limit his visitors this afternoon, but you may come back this evening after he's had an opportunity to rest more."

"Nurse!" Ethan demanded in an imperious tone. "Can you see this young lady?"

"Yes, sir."

"Then I'm not hallucinating?"

The nurse smiled. "No, sir. She's real enough."

"Thank God!"

"Ethan, you must get some rest now," I said. "I'll see you tonight."

"The pity is that I won't see you, but yes, you must come back. Please. I'll still be here."

"I'll be back. I promise," I said as I kissed his cheek and left.

Calvin took me back to the hotel, where I showered and napped briefly. He treated me to supper in a nearby pub and then returned with me to the hospital. We found Ethan still lying in his bed, listening to the evening news. His dinner lay untouched on the bed tray.

"Would you like some help with your meal?" I asked.

He smiled broadly. "What? You're back? You are real then?"

I laughed. "Yes, I'm real. Calvin is here too."

"Cal, you old scoundrel. Are you trying to steal my girl from me while I'm bedridden?"

"Don't worry, man, she's all yours. I'm just watching out for her."

"You can turn that off," Ethan said, nodding toward the television. "And, yes, Jillian, I would like some help with this so-called dinner. They're keeping me on all liquids— not too appetizing, but there should be some Jell-O there at least. I've been wondering how to eat it without spilling it all over myself."

I raised the head of his bed again and proceeded to spoon-feed him, almost as I would Cadence. I tried to keep the conversation light and cheerful. Calvin, following suit, discussed the upcoming football season and the prospects for the Washington Redskins. We managed to steer Ethan's thoughts away from anything morbid or depressing.

As we were preparing to leave, Ethan stopped us.

"Before you go," he said, "I need to tell you both something that I've been mulling over. I've been thinking a lot about God while I've been lying here—I guess coming close to dying will do that to you. Anyway, for many years, I thought I was doing pretty darn well on my own without God. And lately, I'll admit that I've been so blazing mad about my circumstances—the nightmare of the marriage, Jillian leaving, everything—that I didn't much care about anything spiritual. But then, the night before the divorce settlement, I felt so desperate that I cried out to God for his help and have been trying to pray since.

"And then this happened. Calvin and I could have easily died yesterday morning, but I know God spared us. Yes, my arm and my eyes were seriously injured—but even if I never see again, it could have been so much worse. I'm so thankful to be alive. And then, my dear Jillian came back. Another miracle! I can't believe it. God has shown me such mercy. And I don't deserve any of it. It's overwhelming. The thing is—I know I should thank him, but I don't know how to."

"You could live for him now," I said with quiet hope. "You could put him first in your life."

"You're right, I could, and I would like to do that," he said humbly. "Please pray that I will."

"Oh, Ethan, I have and I will."

"Thank you," he said, squeezing my hand.

As I bent down to kiss him good night, my heart filled with grateful joy. The idols in both our lives had been toppled.

⁓❦⁓

The following morning, I returned alone to Ethan's hospital room where I found him in good spirits. At first our conversation centered on Cadence and how she had been faring when I last saw her. That prompted a call to Carter Plantation so that Ethan could speak directly to her and to his aunt Elise, who was anxious for news and relieved to talk with him.

Next, Ethan wanted to hear about all that had transpired in my life since I had left him back in May, and I obliged with a fairly thorough account, including many details that I thought would interest him.

"So, you were with the Brookes all along, after all," he said.

"Yes, but not with the big family in Harrisonburg."

"Why did you write that letter asking me not to look for you?"

"I was afraid of my own feelings. That if I saw you again, I would allow myself to be persuaded to go back with you and live with you."

"I wouldn't have coerced you to, Jillian. I just wanted to make sure that you were provided for. I hated thinking of you out in the world somewhere all on your own."

"You shouldn't have worried about me, Ethan. I can take care of myself. Like I said, I found a good job that I really enjoy."

"I know you are quite the capable young lady, but I worried nonetheless." He shifted uncomfortably in his bed. "Now tell me more about this John Brooke fellow. You've mentioned him quite a bit. Do you like him?"

Ethan's jealousy of John was transparently evident, but I couldn't resist teasing him a little. "Of course," I answered. "There's nothing not to like."

"How old is he and what does he do for a living?"

"He's about twenty-six, and he's serving now as an assistant pastor at the Blue Ridge Community Christian Church, where the preschool is."

"So, is he some kind of a nerd? An unattractive sort of fellow who became a minister through some sort of online degree program or a third-rate Bible college?"

"No, not at all! On the contrary, he graduated from UVA and then earned his MDiv at Princeton. And he's not a nerd or unattractive. He's very handsome, actually. He looks a lot like the actor Jude Law."

"Blast!" Ethan muttered to himself before returning to his questions. "And how effective is he as a pastor? Does he think he's too good to minister to his flock? Is he too busy for them?"

"No, he's very actively involved with the church. He leads

Bible studies and the college-age fellowship, and he's very conscientious about visiting the sick and meeting with anyone who needs ministry."

"Do you like him?"

"Very much. But you already asked me that."

"And you say you spent a good deal of time with him?"

"In the evenings, yes. I attended most of the fellowship meetings with him, and once a week the four of us held our own private Bible study together at home. Then on the other evenings, we studied together."

"What did you study?"

"John and I studied Krio. It's a Creole dialect spoken in Sierra Leone."

"Why the blazes would you study that?"

"He asked me to help him. He plans to be a missionary to Sierra Leone. And then I realized he wanted me to go with him."

"To Sierra Leone?"

"Yes."

"As a missionary with him?"

"Yes."

"Huh," he grunted. "Does he want to marry you?"

"Yes. He did propose to me."

He slammed his good arm down on the bed. "I knew it! Then why are you here? Did you come out of pity? Are you simply doing your Christian duty to visit the infirm?"

"Ethan," I said as soothingly as I could, "you didn't ask me if I accepted his proposal."

"Did you?"

"Of course not."

"Why not? You've described this John fellow as young, handsome, brilliant, and a good man. He loves you and wants to marry you. Why wouldn't you want to marry him?"

"Because I don't love him! And he doesn't love me. We are like brother and sister and that is all. He just thinks I'd make a good partner in ministry. I'm not really happy when I'm with him, and I wouldn't be able to make him happy for long. I don't love him, Ethan," I said, putting my arms around his neck. "I love you! I'm here because I love you and want to be with you. And I'll stay as long as you want me to."

"Do you mean it?" He smiled. "You'll have to stay forever then."

"All right then. Forever it will be."

He tried to kiss me but the cumbersomeness of his bandages interfered. He frowned. "Look at me," he said with disgust. "I'm a wreck of a man."

I gently touched his bandages. "I love *you*, Ethan. Not your appearance or your money or your influence. I love *you*. Nothing else matters."

"Even though I'm covered with scars and may not ever see your lovely face again?"

"Yes, I've told you. Those things don't matter to me."

"I love you so much, Jillian!" He gave a ragged sigh. "But the trouble is that I don't want you to be my nurse. I want you to be my wife. Do you think . . . could you possibly . . . will you marry me now?"

"Of course I will. Nothing would make me happier."

Ethan couldn't see the smile on my face. But when he pulled me close and kissed me, I knew that he had heard the smile in my voice.

I was finally home.

26

Our shared joy only increased the next morning when the doctor removed the bandages from Ethan's eyes, and the first face he beheld was my own. He would have to wear glasses or contact lenses, but that seemed a small hardship to endure for the restoration of his sight. For the rest of his life he would also bear a little scar over one eye, which gave his eyebrow a slightly quizzical lift. I found that scar a constant and endearing reminder of his courage, and compassion, and how close I came to losing him. It became my favorite spot to kiss. Over time, Ethan's burned arm healed, and although the skin never looked quite natural, with rigorous attention to occupational therapy, he regained his full range of motion and strength. The hospital released him in time for us to fly home for Cadence's second birthday.

Ethan and I were quietly married in early October in a

small country church near Middleburg and enjoyed a lovely autumn reception in the garden at Carter Plantation. Cadence made an adorable flower girl while Sharon and Diane served as my bridesmaids and Calvin stood up as best man. All three of our dear friends have since found wonderful spouses of their own and have settled close enough nearby that we can visit them often.

The entire Brooke family attended the wedding, with the exception of John, who was in Dallas at the missionary training school. He did leave that January for Sierra Leone and has been serving there for the last five years. We continue to exchange cordial letters, and I was pleased when Ethan agreed to support, with a substantial ongoing financial contribution, the orphanage at the mission in Freetown. We recently returned from a visit to the mission there and brought home two darling orphans, whom we named Katie and Christian and adopted as our own.

I had previously presented Cadence with twin baby brothers, Britan and Colton, close to her fourth birthday, and we hope to continue to expand the Remington clan by both birth and adoption in the years to come.

I am kept very busy in caring for the children and being a good wife and life partner to my beloved husband. Even though we live with Aunt Elise at Carter Plantation, we make frequent visits to Keswick Hall, where children's laughter now fills the halls, banishing any haunting memories of a woman in white.

Ethan continues to oversee his thriving international

telecommunications company, and although from time to time he invests in quality film productions, most of his discretionary income goes to supporting our local church, the mission in Sierra Leone, and various philanthropic trusts, particularly those that benefit orphaned children. As demanding as his work responsibilities are, he always finds time to devote to our family, and he never ceases to invest his time and talents in service and gratitude to God.

My life has taken some surprising twists and turns, and yet through it all I have sensed God's guiding hand with me on the journey. I am constantly thankful for his presence. I am also thankful for the young woman who chose to give me life. I sometimes wonder what it cost her to leave me in that hospital and if she thinks about what may have happened to her little daughter. I like to believe that she prayed for my care and for my future.

I hope she knows that God's eye is on the sparrow—especially the smallest ones.

A Note from the Author

This book is intended as my homage to the classic story of *Jane Eyre* by Charlotte Brontë. I approached this adaptation with some trepidation because I'm well aware of the criticisms which it could engender among Brontë purists. This book was not written for the purists, however, but for three other types of readers. The first type—like me—is the lover of the classics who enjoys contemporary adaptations and is intrigued by finding the similarities and differences with the original story, as well as by conjecturing how the author will work things out in a modern setting. The second is the type who likes to read romantic suspense. And the third is the person who has not yet read *Jane Eyre*. My great hope is that this reader will enjoy my story enough to be inspired to read the original classic.

I am grateful to Debra White Smith, the author of a series of contemporary treatments of Jane Austen's books, for her inspiration and personal encouragement. Thanks are in order to the editors and staff of Revell, my new publishing house, and my agent Joyce Hart, who introduced me to them. I'd also like to thank my daughter, Katherine Craddock, friends Inece Bryant, Diane DeMark, Elizabeth Sheridan, and Karla Vernon, who kindly read through and made suggestions on the first draft of the book, and especially my mother Betty Morey, who is an incomparable editor and proofreader. Thanks to my church, the King's Chapel, for encouragement and prayers, and to my husband, Bill, and our family, who endured long stretches of time when I sat apart at my computer and lived in the realm of the imagination. Finally, thanks to my readers for your enthusiasm and support. Your letters and emails mean so much, and I really appreciate hearing from you. You can contact me at inklingsauthor@yahoo.com or visit my website at www .inklingsauthor.com.

Soli Deo Gloria

Melanie Morey Jeschke
Vienna, Virginia
Spring 2009

Melanie M. Jeschke is the author of the Oxford Chronicles series, including *Inklings*, *Expectations*, and *Evasions*, as well as numerous travel articles. An honors graduate of the University of Virginia and former home-educator, she currently teaches British literature and lectures in a variety of educational, professional, and community settings. Jeschke has traveled extensively in the UK, where she sets her stories. A mother of nine, she resides in Northern Virginia with her family and husband Bill Jeschke, senior pastor of The King's Chapel.